Forever My Home

TYLER CREEK SERIES

ROXIE CLARKE

WRITE
FREE
PRESS

Introduction

Hi! Thanks for picking up *Forever My Home*.
I appreciate it.
To stay updated on sales and new releases you
can sign up for my newsletter at
www.roxieclarke.com.
Catch up with me on Facebook or Instagram.

One

Lettie

"Take it! Take another little piece of my heart now baby," I scream-sing along to Janis Joplin, a constant companion on my cross-country trip from Braverton to Tyler Creek. Before I left home, my best friend Maryann made sure I had approximately one billion hours of music to listen to while I drove my hunter green 2013 Outback filled with all my earthly possessions to my new home. On CD, because we're just that old and because we don't trust streaming services to always work or for there to be a decent cell signal.

Case in point, my GPS has been *rerouting...rerouting...* for the last five miles through these dry foothills broken up by roadside groves of low hanging trees casting shadows against the dusty paved road, blocking out the noonday sun. The change in lighting has me squinting one minute and opening my eyes as wide as possible the next. I'd given up on flipping my sunglasses down off the top of my head and then pushing them back up every quarter mile.

I turn the music down so I can see better and focus on finding a sign indicating I've arrived at the driveway to the Enchanted Cavern Cottages – the woodland vacation retreat my great aunt Lettie, my namesake, left me in her will.

The expectation is a secluded gravel driveway leading off into the woods. At least that's what the photos in the packet Aunt Lettie's lawyer had sent me shows. But I'm just not finding anything that matches the pictures and, to be honest, I'm not sure I'm even on the right road.

"My queendom for a paper map," I

mutter and turn the music completely off with a hard press of the button. Glancing behind me in the rearview, all I can see is the dust cloud in my wake, but since I haven't seen another vehicle for half an hour at least, I slow way down, scrutinizing both sides of the road.

As I drive around the next curve, I spot a person on a horse, leading four other people on horseback along a roadside trail.

I approach and roll down my passenger side window, leaning across the front seat littered with CD's, granola bar wrappers, a few ChapSticks, and a bag of McDonald's trash.

"Hey there," I say, giving the lead guy, an attractive man with tanned skin who is wearing a black cowboy hat, black Western shirt, tight dark jeans, and brown boots, a wave and my most neighborly smile.

He tips his hat up and ducks down to see into my car. "Howdy. You need directions?"

I chuckle. "That obvious, huh?"

The cowboy grins. "It's easy to get lost out here. And a GPS will lead you into a lake if you're not careful. Where ya headed?"

"The Enchanted Cavern Cottages."

He furrows his brow. "You know they're

closed, right? Have been for half a year or so."

I nod. "I do. I'm the new owner."

"Are you now?" He twists in the saddle and points behind him. "You're almost there. The drive is on your left. There's a great big willow tree just before the turn off. The sign fell over during a strong storm last December."

"Ah, thank you. I've been looking for a sign." I smirk. "For the cottages, not like, if taking on this adventure is a mistake or not."

His horse bends its head down and starts chewing on a patch of scraggly high grass. The man gently tugs on the reins.

I give him a thumbs up. "Thanks for the directions. I'll let you go."

"Anytime. I'm Henry, my place is on up the road, the next drive after the cottages. Welcome to Tyler Creek."

"Thanks, Henry. I'm Lettie."

His eyes light up with recognition. "You must be related to Miss Lettie who owned the cottages when I was a kid."

An image of a younger Henry, dressed in his cowboy gear, perched on a gray pony leading another cream-colored pony behind dredges up from my memory. I'd only been to Tyler Creek once when I was a pre-teen and despite my great aunt telling me I should get outside and enjoy the property, I'd spent most of my visit in her guest room reading. I'd turned down the offer to ride ponies with the neighbor kid.

"Yep. She was my great aunt. On my mother's side." Lettie never had any children to leave the cottages to, but I was still surprised when she'd willed them to me. And thankful. My life was in a downward spiral and complete upheaval was in order. Like a cross-country move.

Henry tips his hat. "My condolences. I have fond memories of her and that apple pie she used to make."

"It's a family recipe," I say. "When I get settled, I'll do some baking and have you over." *Okay.* Pretty bold of you, Lettie, to already be inviting a man to your house, but what good is starting over if you can't be a bit bolder than you were in your old life?

He chuckles and his horse shifts to the side, probably anxious to get moving. "That sounds wonderful, but I imagine it'll be a while."

"That bad, huh?" He did say the place had been shuttered for six months. "As long as there aren't a bunch of mice and rats skittering about, I think I can handle it."

Henry gives his horse a tap with his boot heel. "Good luck. Left turn right after the big willow tree."

"Got it. Thanks again." I give him another thumbs up and raise the window.

I wait until Henry and his group are past me before driving off, so I don't stir up dust in their faces.

Sure enough, two minutes later I spot the great big willow and a gravel driveway. It's overgrown with brambles, vines, and tall clumpy weeds. Nothing a weed whacker and some determination can't fix.

I turn onto the drive and make my way into the woods, the dappled sunlight through the trees casting pleasant, lazy shadows onto the hood of my car.

My shoulders un-scrunch and a thrill goes through me. After four days of driving, I'm finally here, beginning a new and hopefully more exciting chapter of my life.

Things in Braverton had been awful for a

long time and had only gotten worse in the last three months. My job of twenty years as the live-in manager of a ten-room B&B ended without warning when an out-of-town investor bought the property with plans to demolish the building. I was left with no job and no place to live, and due to a horrible break up that ended in bankruptcy two years ago, my credit is so bad I can't even rent a studio apartment. Maryann would've let me move in with her and her husband, Luis, but that wasn't a permanent solution, or even a weeklong solution. Couch surfing at forty-four years old is something I can't bring myself to do.

"No matter what's around this corner," I say to myself. "It'll be different."

I move forward into a clearing, what used to be a small auxiliary parking area if I remember correctly. The sheer number of massive, taller-than-my-car dandelions and thistles erupting through the gravel grabs hold of the thrill from a moment before and chokes it out.

My tires mow a path through the weeds, vegetation scraping against the sides of the car, no doubt scratching the paint job. Then the car abruptly sinks down into a deep rut that jars my teeth.

I ease the front tires out of the rut, only to then drive over a rigid mound of *something*.

A pile of gravel? Dirt? Dead bodies?

I don't get out to check. That's for later Lettie to discover.

Forging ahead, the ground levels out, but the weeds don't abate. In fact, a tangle of blackberry briars and honeysuckle vines join the party to my left. I edge the car to the right, searching my memory for bodies of water on the property. The Outback can likely handle a drive through a creek, but not survive a plunge into a pond. Henry had been kidding about the lake, right? I don't recall a lake.

Keeping to the right proves to be the better choice, as to my forward left a weathered post with a rotten gate door hanging by one hinge juts out of the brambles. There isn't a post or fence of any kind that I can see on the right, so I continue down what I'm hoping is the circular drive that passes by each of the eight cottages and the main house which serves as the office and my residence.

Finally, there's a break in the weeds on the right and I realize the gravel drive is *over there*, and not what I've been tearing through. Was this where the fenced off fire pit and picnic area had been? A memory of roasting marshmallows sitting on a halved log bench comes to mind. I guess I did venture outside a few times back then.

"For crying out loud," I mutter and get the car onto the actual road. First order of business is to get all this vegetation torn down because there is no way I'll be able to make this drive in the dark and I'd planned on going into Tyler Creek proper to pick up some groceries and cleaning supplies this evening.

A moment later, there is a marked change in the light and the sun blinds me as I pass through an opening in the surrounding trees, before I'm thrown back into the deep shade of the forest. Then, suddenly, there is a cottage next to me, three more to my forward right, and the main house directly in front of me.

I stop the car, gaping, and burst into tears.

Two

Lettie

The first cottage is in shambles. The two steps up to the sagging porch, if you can even call that thing a porch, are caved in at the middle. Where the flower boxes underneath the front windows to either side of the door once held flowers, they're presently filled with moss and toadstools and coated on the face with a slimy pink *something*. Yellow jacket nests have taken over the space underneath the boxes.

Bees. I can deal with bees. I've even dreamt of setting up my own hives and selling the honey and other locally produced goods in the office in the small gift shop area I have planned. Yellow jackets were not part of my honeyed fantasy.

The roof on this cottage is more blue tarp than roof and I can only imagine the inside is an ideal breeding ground for toxic black mold.

The porch and the roof on the second cottage are in better shape, but the gutters on each side are hanging off, having succumbed to the weight of compacted mud, pine needles, and… *is that poison ivy?*

I wipe the tears from my face with the back of my hand and unplug my cell phone from the charger. I need Maryann to convince me I can do this thing that I very much don't want to do at the moment. The display on my phone reads *calling…calling*, but it can't connect because there's no signal. That deluxe data package I bought is as useless out here as I am. How am I going to survive until the internet gets set up 'whenever we can send a guy out' as the man on the phone had told me last week? I bite back a scream and fling my phone onto the messy passenger seat with a scowl.

Driving past the third and fourth cottages which are in various and myriad other states of disrepair, I decide I'm not even going to check out the cottages on the other side of the property. They're situated deeper in the woods and sure to be crawling with critters.

A critter encounter will send me over the edge.

I park my car to the side of the office/residence and get out to take a look, leaving my belongings behind in case it's necessary to flee from raccoon or opossum squatters.

The one-story bungalow style house is rundown. Peeling exterior faded yellow paint same as the cottages, the once white windowsills splintered to reveal dry graying wood underneath, and about half of the cedar shingles are missing from the roof, but there are no visible holes and I guess that's about all I can hope for.

I find the key on my ring and put my foot on the bottom step, testing that it'll hold, before climbing up the next three. This porch is filthy and in need of a scrubbing and fresh paint, but it's stable and level. The swing at the far end, one I remember curling up on in the evening after dinner to watch for lightning bugs, hangs on rusty chains and the yellow and orange floral cushion is stained with mildew.

How long since Aunt Lettie ran this place? She passed at the age of ninety-six, so it was likely she hadn't overseen operations since the early 2000s. The lawyer said a property management company had taken over maintenance and renting out the cottages until last fall. My expectation was things would be dated and dusty and need some cosmetic repairs.

I have half a mind to sue the pants off them for allowing things to get this bad! The fact that they were taking my aunt's money should be considered fraud.

I unlock the pristine silver padlock on the front door, its newness mocking me. A musty smell wafts from inside as I push the door open wide. Dust motes swirl in the air and float down to the scuffed wood floors, shimmering in the beams of sunlight shining in through the four tall windows in the reception area. The room is empty except for an orange laminate top reception desk and three black particle board IKEA bookshelves along the wood paneled wall behind it.

Hoping that the power got turned on like I requested, I flip the switch on the wall to the right of the doorway. The overhead light and ceiling fan come to life.

Buoyed by that good fortune, I walk through the front room toward the kitchen at the back of the house.

After a stutter, the water from the tap at the kitchen sink flows dirty and then clear into the almond-colored porcelain basin. I cup my hands under the water and take a sip. Drinkable, not even a funny chlorine aftertaste.

Tears well in my eyes and I swipe them away with wet fingers, laughing to myself.

I take stock of the kitchen. The linoleum flooring is yellowed, but intact. There is a thick layer of dust on top of the orange laminate counters, the avocado green appliances, and the little two-seater table and chairs under the window that looks out into the woods behind the house. I grin at the table "printed" with vintage newspaper clippings. Aunt Lettie had gotten the furniture for free when the Wendy's in Bentonville did a remodel. She'd been so proud of that deal.

"I got something for nothing!" she'd said, relating the story to me while she rolled out dough for her famous apple pie.

The brown carpeted hallway off the kitchen leads to the bathroom and the two bedrooms. I run my fingertips over the tan wallpaper with gold flourishes as I make my way to the bathroom. It's peeling back at the seams ever so slightly, but otherwise the wallpaper is in good shape. The vintage thrift store owner in Maryann would absolutely have a fit over this late-seventies time capsule.

I peek into the bathroom. It's in need of a good cleaning, of course. The beige tub/shower combo, sink, and toilet all have rust stains. The linoleum is the same as the kitchen in pattern and condition. Above the sink, the mirrored front medicine cabinet is cloudy around the edges and has a piece of duct tape holding the magnet latch on.

There's a stiff mildew-stained pink bath towel hanging on the towel bar next to the tub which I'm absolutely not touching until I have triple latex gloved my hands.

Down the hall, the bedrooms are identical, save the first has a full-sized bed and the second a twin sized. Both need the mattresses replaced, although the simple metal frames and box springs seem fine.

I take a deep breath. The house is habitable. Small miracles.

Now that I know what I'm up against as far as my home is concerned, I head out to my car to fetch the cardboard box of cleaning supplies I have on hand out of the back and then make return trips for my vacuum, mop, and mop bucket.

Fishing a red scrunchie out of my denim capris pocket, I put my bottle blond shoulder length hair up into a ponytail and get to work on the bathroom.

An hour later, the bathroom and both bedrooms are clean. I've claimed the full-sized bedroom as my own, spreading two sleeping bags on top of the old mattress for the time being. Since there isn't a dresser, I hang up what I can in the small closet and leave the rest folded in my powder pink hard-shell suitcase.

I wander into the kitchen with my box of cleaning supplies and open the fridge to find the ubiquitous box of baking soda, a half a stick of margarine on a white melamine saucer, and a sticky mess that looks like a two-liter of cola has pooled and dripped from the top shelf down to the second and into the crisper drawers at the bottom. It's only a guess, though, as there isn't a bottle in sight. *Ick.*

"That's a whole lot of can't even right now," I say, setting the cardboard box on the dusty counter behind me. I pull out a bottle of 409 and shake it. It's almost out, as is the Windex. And I could use a few rolls of paper towel since most of my rags are filthy and I'm too chicken to venture down to the basement to check out the laundry machine situation.

My stomach growls obscenely loud in the empty house, reminding me that I require and deserve food, preferably of no nutritional value but with maximum emotional soothing powers.

I redo my ponytail and do a quick armpit sniff check, determining that I'm only slightly stinky and that the residents of Tyler Creek can deal with it. Then I'm back in my car, happy that the driveway is more apparent from this side of things.

I avoid looking at the cottages and crank up Janis on the stereo, mentally making a list of all the stuff I need to buy to get myself through the next twenty-four hours.

Three

Henry

I finish getting the horses watered and in their stalls for a cool afternoon rest before I head over to my utility shed to load up the back of my truck with my landscaping equipment. I pitch in several sturdy yard waste totes to make hauling debris away easier, the mower, weed whacker, hedge trimmer, chain saw, rake, and a sharp, long machete for hacking at blackberry brambles. I've always got two or three pair of thick work gloves in the cab of the truck, so no need to grab those. I consider taking my hat with mosquito netting, but it's been so dry lately that the mosquitoes haven't been too bothersome. My cowboy hat oughta do and my clothing is already dusty and sweaty from the noon day trail ride and will protect my skin from the sun and scratchy vegetation.

After the encounter with my new neighbor, Lettie, I got to thinking what an overgrown mess her property must be. From the road you can hardly see down the driveway; it can only be worse as you get deeper into the woods.

Our shared woods that I use these very same tools on to keep them from encroaching on my pasture. Offering Lettie good luck in dealing with her rundown property wasn't very neighborly of me. Not when I knew what she was in for, and she didn't.

With the truck loaded, I drive down the road not even a quarter mile and turn onto the gravel driveway. I decide to make my presence known to her before I begin hacking away at things with my machete. The poor woman has had enough of a shock for one day.

"Oh, boy." I whistle. It appears that Lettie

missed the bend in the road and had herself a four-wheeling adventure through what I recall was once the native plant garden and communal fire pit area.

I stick to the actual road, although I can see where she might have missed it down low in her station wagon.

My heart sinks when the cottages come into view. I shake my head, guilt flooding my body. I'd thought of this property as an eyesore and nuisance for years, but figured if people were still living here that it couldn't be this bad. I wish I'd checked to make sure that the management company was doing their job, because they'd clearly swindled sweet Miss Lettie out of her money. These cottages are uninhabitable.

Lettie's car isn't parked at the house, which thankfully looks shabby but livable, so I drive around the circle past the other cottages. No car there either. I wouldn't blame her if she took one look at this place and went back wherever she came from.

But, on the off chance she does return, especially if she comes back after dark, the least I can do is clear the driveway for her.

Three hot and humid hours later, the road

to the cottages is obvious and there's four feet of space on either side. I've removed enough debris to fill all the totes I brought to over-flowing and raked the remainder into manage-able piles I'll come back for later.

I take off my right glove and wipe the sweat from my brow with the back of my hand. My busted knee from my rodeo days is aching like nobody's business, which is al-ways my cue to quit for the day.

There's one last thing I want to do before I go. I'd extricated the Enchanted Cavern Cot-tages sign from a gnarly mess of briars and vines early on. Now I stand it upright, it's about waist high, and drag it over to the dri-veway entrance and prop it against the trunk of an oak tree.

Satisfied I've done all I can do to be helpful for today, I climb back into my truck, take off my left glove and place the pair on the floor behind the passenger side seat, and head home.

I grin thinking about the look of surprise on Lettie's pretty face when she sees my handiwork. Yeah, yeah. I noticed she's pleasant to look at. Would I have gone to this trouble if my new neighbor was a man? Not likely. I'd wait until a man asked to borrow my tools before I offered to help him out. Still neighborly, but not quite as eager to please.

And if I'm being honest with myself, it's been a while since I've been interested in a woman. It's not often people in my age range move to Tyler Creek. No offense to the born and bred TC women, but I've known them since elementary school and dated them in high school and in my twenties. Never did click with anyone.

Yep. Lettie's arrival stirs things up a little bit. In a good way.

Four

Lettie

I park my car on Tyler's Way in front of a darling community theater, noting that a production of *Disney's Beauty and the Beast Jr.* is happening at the end of next month. Right before school starts, I suppose. What I'm not expecting to see on a small-town theater marquee is that the production is directed by *Broadway's own Hunter Lowe!* And then in parentheses, (Yes, the New York Broadway). If I can manage to ever get to downtown Tyler

Creek without getting lost four times, then I'll have to check out the show.

I blow my bangs out of my eyes and slide my red vintage cat's eye sunglasses on. The day has only gotten hotter and the purple and pink wave petunias in the huge hanging baskets on the light poles along the street are as wilted as I feel.

Still, the second time I got turned around and asked for directions a nice old man out for a country stroll with his hound dog told me the best way to beat the heat is to have a frozen custard from Buster's, which checks all the boxes of my treat criteria.

He'd told me that Buster's is right on Tyler's Way, so in theory, if I walk up one side of the street and down the other, I'm likely to find this frozen custard Mecca. Nutritious groceries and cleaning supplies can wait until later.

I pass by a ton of cute shops that I'll definitely have to explore post-custard. A cheese shop and a year-round Christmas shop especially catch my eye.

As I walk, I'm greeted by friendly smiles and 'afternoons' from other people out and about. I get a catch in my throat, thinking about Braverton, the small town filled with kind people I'd left behind. It's not nearly as humid in Braverton, Oregon, but there is something to be said for the Southern charm and slower pace of Tyler Creek.

I spot Buster's across the street and hurry to the crosswalk, which surprisingly, cars stop at to yield to pedestrians. All right, another tick in the pro column for this small town.

Buster's Custard is a stand, with some picnic tables off to the side. I'd been hoping for some air conditioning, but it is what it is. Not to mention, I should try acclimating to the higher temps here.

The line is four people deep at the counter and a small crowd to the right waits for their orders.

I scan the menu board up above the counter windows. I've never had frozen custard before since it's not big in Oregon, although I know there are a few places that sell it.

After determining I have no idea what to get, I tap the brunette woman in front of me on the shoulder.

She turns and smiles, her eyebrows raised.

"Hi, I'm new to town," I say, returning her smile. "What's good?"

Her eyes go wide. "It's all good, but my favorite is the lemon crumble concrete with a raspberry drizzle."

The handsome, bespectacled, tall man next to her chimes in, "But if you're a chocolate person, the rocky road concrete is the way to go."

A man in a mint-green polo shirt in front of him turns and says, "There's nothing wrong with ordering plain vanilla in a cup, either. It's a common order."

The brunette nods. "It's what we're getting the kids." She points to a willowy teenage girl, a preteen girl doing pirouettes, and a baby in a stroller next to the longest picnic table. An adult woman, a few years younger than me, sits with them animatedly making faces at the baby and getting it to giggle.

A woman with a cute pixie cut in front of the brunette leans around her. "You can't trust him, he's a sugar hating dentist. I personally like a cherry dipped chocolate cone and I'd say out of all of us I'm the most knowledgeable when it comes to frozen treats."

"Oh?" I ask. "Do you work in the food business?"

She shakes her head. "No, I own the community theater, but I eat a lot of ice cream and custard. Way more than any of these peeps."

Everyone but the vanilla-in-a-cup dentist guy laughs. The rugged looking man next to her puts his arm around her shoulders and gives her a kiss on the top of her head.

I join in the laughing. "You all are not making this choice any easier."

The brunette asks, "Are you new in town as in you've moved here?"

All of them look at me expectantly.

"Yes. Just today, in fact." *And I'm not sure I'm staying because I'm a big wimp who's in over her head.*

"Well then you've got time to try everything," she says, then lowers her voice to a whisper, "but the lemon crumble concrete is what you should start with."

Everyone laughs again and then it's cherry dipped chocolate lady and her fella's turn to order.

"I'm Monica." The woman in front of me extends her hand and I shake it.

"Lettie," I say.

She gestures to the man next to her. "And this is my husband, Hunter."

He nods, his glasses sliding down his nose. He pushes them up. "Pleased to meet you."

"You wouldn't be *Broadway's Hunter Lowe*, would you?" I tease.

Hunter chuckles and unfurls a dramatic bow. "One and the same."

Monica rolls her eyes. "I co-own the theater with my best friend Darcie and teach high school drama. The guy next to her is her hubby, Jack." She points to the dentist. "This is Miles, the best dentist in Tyler Creek and over there by Darcie's girls and my son, is Miles' girlfriend, Heather."

"Wow, you've got quite the tight-knit group," I say. "It's nice you all can get together for custard on a random Wednesday afternoon."

"It's my thirty-third birthday," Miles says by way of explanation. "I like your t-shirt. Bend, Oregon is a place I'd like to visit when I do the Pacific Crest Trail next year."

I pull the t-shirt away from my body and

peer down at it like I don't know what it looks like. Yep. Still a blue t-shirt with a red outline of mountains and the words Bend, OR on it. At least if I'm going to be awkward my shirt is relatively clean.

"Thanks. Bend is great, you definitely should check it out."

"Is Oregon where you moved from?" Monica asks, as Darcie comes over to stand by her and Miles moves up in line to order.

"Yeah. Braverton. It's a small town outside of Portland."

My cheeks heat as I see Monica's next question forming on her lips.

"Cool. Are you out here for work or… change of pace?"

I force a confident smile. "I, um, inherited the Enchanted Cavern Cottages from my great aunt Lettie when she passed."

Recognition flares in Hunter, Monica, and Darcie's eyes.

"Oh, wow," Monica says. "That's…"

"You're up," Miles says and walks over to wait next to Jack.

I welcome the distraction from continuing to discuss my Unenchanted Cruddy Cottages.

But Darcie hangs back. "You poor thing," she says, patting my shoulder.

"Hey, Mon?" Darcie asks her friend.

Monica waves me up. "Great minds, Darce. Lettie, we'll get your custard. You must be putting on a brave face."

Tears well in my eyes and I blink them back, thankful for the sunglasses. "That's so nice of you, but we just met. It's not necessary."

Monica shrugs. "But we've met, which makes us acquaintances on our way to being friends."

"Okay," I say, unscrunching my shoulders. "I'll take that lemon thing you're having."

Darcie gestures toward Heather. "Heather is a former resident of the cottages if you need someone to commiserate with." She loops her arm around mine and drags me in the direction of the picnic tables.

"Heather, this is Lettie. She's the new owner of the cabin cottage thingy's you used to live in."

The animated woman sighs loudly and makes a pouty face and then narrows her eyes at me for a second then throws her shoulders back and sits up tall. "You got this." She circles her hand in front of me. "Your energy can handle whatever it takes to get this job done. I can feel it. I can see it."

Darcie clears her throat. "Heather has recently discovered she can see auras."

I raise my eyebrows. "Okay…"

Heather cackles. "And I swear it's a gift not the effects of the toxic mold exposure from the cottages you now own. Promise. For realsies."

A giggle bubbles up and out of me. "You know what?" I say. "I'm going to believe that you're right."

She claps her hands. "Yay. Because, really, what's the alternative? A descent into madness? A funkarific funk? No, thanks!"

Everyone who'd been waiting on the custard comes over and grabs a seat around the picnic table.

Monica hands me a concoction kind of like a Dairy Queen Blizzard but made with custard instead of soft serve. "Well, you're smiling, so Heather must have read your aura and lightened the mood. She's good like that."

I smile at Heather. "Yes. Mood lightened

and improved." I gesture with my cup. "Thanks for this, Monica. I appreciate it."

"Welcome to TC, Lettie." She sits down next to Hunter at the table and motions for me to join them.

I take a bite of the custard and it is so good. Decadent, creamy, and cool as it slides down my throat. Another check in the Tyler Creek pro column. Actually, double checks because what could have been just a bright blip in an otherwise crummy day, has become a chance to meet nice locals and get an unexpected pep talk. Speaking of, a call to Maryann before I head back to the cottages will keep this momentum going.

When I finish my custard I bid my new acquaintances goodbye, promising to attend *Beauty and the Beast Jr.* on opening night and thanking Miles for the fifteen percent off teeth cleaning coupon.

I call Maryann on my walk to my car.

"You made it!" Maryann says. "Did you just get in? According to my calculations, you were supposed to arrive in Tyler Creek this morning?"

"Hello, to you too." I grin. "It's good to

hear your voice and thanks for keeping tabs on me."

"It's what we do, Let," Maryann says.

"Hola, Leticia," Maryann's husband, Luis, says into the phone.

"Hola."

"She says hola, honey," Maryann says. "So, tell me about Tyler Creek. Is it what you expected?"

I sigh. "It's worse and better than I thought. The property my aunt left me is a dump. Like, maybe should be condemned."

Maryann gasps. "No. I'm so sorry. That's the pits. But there's some better?"

"Yes, silver lining is the country is beautiful and the people are friendly. I have an attractive cowboy neighbor. Oh, and frozen custard is the bomb. You and Luis should totally open a stand in Braverton. It would kill."

"Mm hmm. I stopped listening when you said hot cowboy neighbor."

I giggle like I'm fifteen and not almost forty-five. "I didn't say hot, I said attractive."

"So, he's not hot?" She laughs.

"No, he totally is."

"What are you going to do about the cottages? Do you have a decent place to live?" Maryann asks.

"The residence isn't too bad. Just dirty, so I can handle it. The other stuff, like gutter repairs and roof replacement...I have a lot of how-to YouTube videos in my future. That is, after the internet gets connected whenever the installer can get around to it. There's no cell reception up there. That's why I didn't call until I was in town."

"Ugh. So, you can't even work on the new website while you're at home, huh?"

"Nope. But it'll give me a chance to come into town more often. There are lots of cute cafes to hang out in and one of the women I met today said the town library is decent."

"Yes! I love a library. Any good vintage shopping?"

"Not that I've seen so far, although there is a year-round Christmas store."

"Amazing."

"Once I'm settled you and Luis will have to come out for a visit," I say, having arrived at my car.

"Can't wait," Maryann says.

I unlock the car with my fob and climb into the front seat, glancing up at the theatre marquee. It's even funnier now that I know all the people behind it. "Okay, I've gotta go, but I'll call you tomorrow or the next day."

"Good luck, Let. Love you. Bye."

"Love you, too. Bye," I say, hoping all this luck people keep wishing me comes to pass.

Five

Lettie

It's getting near dusk when I load my car up with the last bag of groceries and cleaning supplies, ready to make my way home.

Determined to not get outrageously lost like I did on my way into town, I hyper focus on my surroundings, noting landmarks like, *spot where I talked to the old man with a hound dog, super narrow bridge over Tyler Creek, yard with one million whirly gigs and wind chimes,* and finally, *hot cowboy neighbor getting his mail from his mailbox.* Yes, fine, hot is the better word for how Henry looks and that last one is maybe more of an observation and less of a landmark as Henry standing by his mailbox isn't permanent.

I pull alongside him and lower the passenger side window. "Hey, neighbor."

He tips his hat at me. A different hat than earlier and as a matter of fact, an entire fresh outfit – dark blues this time.

"Hey, neighbor. Did you take a trip into town?" Henry tucks his mail under his arm and leans into the window.

"I did. Had some Buster's Custard. Met a bunch of super cool locals and bought the Kroger out of cleaning supplies."

He gives me a warm chuckle. "Yeah, I reckon I should've warned you that the property was in a bad way."

"It's okay. I live to clean another day and look; I made it back here on the first go!" I cringe and then laugh. "Although, I aimed to come at the property from the other direction. But whatever, I got myself back in the general area and that's the best I can hope for."

"Well, I propped your sign up against a

tree, so you shouldn't miss the driveway no matter which way you're driving."

I smile up at him. "That's so sweet of you. Thanks."

"It was no problem. I should've offered to do it earlier." Henry smirks. "You got a pen in there? Let me give you my number in case you need anything. I should've thought of that earlier too."

His number? I dig around in my purse for a pen and come up with one I apparently took from the Braverton Credit Union. Oops!

I hand the pen to Henry, and he looks through his mail until he finds a flier from Miles the Dentist that proclaims he's taking new patients.

"There's some blank space on the back here," Henry says and scribbles the pen to get the ink going before writing down his number.

I accept the flier even though I technically can't call him from my house since my cell doesn't get service up here.

"I guess you could've put your number directly in my phone or called me from yours," I say, chuckling.

He shakes his head. "I suspect I could've.

Although, my cell phone is older than dirt and the service is unreliable." He nods to the flier. "That there is my landline number. You may want to get the landline hooked up at your place too, just in case."

"Good idea, the phone company will be out sometime in the near future to get the internet going. I'm sure there's some package that includes a landline too."

"I'm sure." Henry rubs a knuckle back and forth across the bottom of his stubbly chin, grinning. "Probably called the old folks and people who live in the boonies package."

"Catchy name. You can go into advertising if the cowboy thing doesn't work out."

The corner of his mouth hitches up. "Hey, have you had dinner yet? I was just about to sit down to a bowl of chili and cornbread. You're welcome to join me."

"Of course, the cowboy makes chili," I say, laughing.

He tips his hat at me again. "Sometimes clichés are comforting. And I make darn good chili."

"I'll bet you do." I point my thumb over my shoulder to the backseat full of supplies.

"I'll have to take a raincheck, though. I've got a date with my disgusting kitchen that I need to get started on sooner than later."

"Alrighty, raincheck then," Henry says, knocking twice on the side of the car. "I'll let you go. Have a good one."

"You too, Henry. Enjoy your dinner."

He nods and backs away from the car. "Will do."

I leave the window lowered as I drive down the road to my place, the scent of gardenias wafting into the car from somewhere nearby. I spot the willow tree and, sure enough, to my right is the Enchanted Cavern Cottages sign propped against another large tree. I turn into my driveway and slam on the brakes, which sounds more dramatic than it is because I'm going, like, two miles an hour.

"Hot cowboy Henry," I say aloud, marveling at the driveway that had been overgrown earlier today now free of weeds and vines and blackberry brambles. Driving toward the turn up ahead where things went horribly awry on my first attempt, the road is cleared and easy to maneuver.

This had to have taken him all afternoon.

I've got to get the kitchen clean just so I can start baking the twenty apple pies Henry deserves for helping me out.

I let out a deep breath as I easily make my way toward the cottages. Yeah, they still look awful, but with the yard debris cleared and the fading light, I can almost pretend the property appears as it did when I was a kid.

I park next to the residence and get out of the car, pressing the trunk unlock button on my key fob. The hatchback rises and so does the hair on the back of my neck. I'm not alone. I look over my shoulder, checking for a squirrel or opossum. Something was skittering behind me from the gravel driveway into the woods.

Or I'm having auditory hallucinations.

There's nothing there now. "Whatever it is, is more afraid of you than you are of it," I say out loud in my most convincing grown lady voice.

I hurry to unload the car, carrying as much as I can in as few trips as I can. After the last bags, I slam the hatchback closed and make a dash for the front door. I can still sense something out there, their eyes boring into my back.

With a shiver, I bump the door closed with my hip, dump the bags on the floor and lock the measly single lock on the doorknob. No wonder there was a padlock on the door earlier.

I scooch the bags over to the edge of the reception desk with my foot and then walk around it to plug in the lamp sitting on top of the counter.

Tucked underneath next to a power outlet is a landline, complete with a black cordless phone still nestled in its charging cradle. I pick the phone up and hold it to my ear, not expecting to hear a dial tone, but there it is loud and clear. I giggle at my paranoia. No one is watching me. I'm simply not used to being in the woods. Braverton is a small town, but only eight miles from Portland, so it has plenty of city-adjacent nighttime sounds. It's never truly quiet like it is here.

Comforted by the working landline and knowing Henry and 911 are only a call away, I get started on this evening's entertainment, cleaning the gross fridge with an assist from ABBA.

"I am a cleaning queen," I sing-scream, tossing a cup of hot soapy water onto the sticky top shelf and watching it run down the back of the fridge, following the path of the hopefully Coke because if it's not then I might hurl. "Old and mean, almost three times seventeeeeeen. Oh ohhhhh."

Six

Lettie

The next morning, I roll out of bed, having slept well despite the sagging mattress, and get dressed in the same capris from the day before and a clean t-shirt, this time a hot pink V-neck.

I wash my face and brush my teeth, returning my toiletries to the spic and span medicine cabinet and then put my hair in a ponytail.

Grabbing a mini-notebook and a regular

ink pen not stolen from a credit union out of my purse, I head outside.

If I've learned one thing about myself, it's that making a list motivates me and activates a part of my brain that believes I can accomplish skills way beyond what I have ever accomplished before.

I begin at the front of cottage four, the closest one to the house. It needs a power wash, new exterior paint, and one window box replaced. I walk the perimeter. The windows are in decent shape and the roof is good. The shingles on four and three appear to have been done more recently than two and one. I jiggle the railing and bounce lightly on the stairs as I move onto the porch. All sturdy enough. Now to face the inside.

I hold my breath and turn the knob. I'd located keys to cottages five through eight in a drawer behind the reception desk but hadn't found any for the first four.

The door opens easily into the front room. It smells stale, but not moldy or musty, which is great. Dust motes tickle my nose as I enter, and I sneeze twice into my elbow. At my feet, the wood floor has a quarter circle scrape across it caused by the bottom of the door, which isn't catching on it now. This is something I recognize from all my years in Oregon. The door swells in the winter and contracts in the summer. July Lettie is gonna let October Lettie deal with this minor problem.

I add it to the list in my notebook, along with the crumbling mortar around the brick base underneath the woodstove, and a ratty loveseat and armchair that need removing and replaced.

Down the hallway there is a teeny tiny kitchen on the left that has enough room for an apartment size fridge, a two-burner stove top, small stainless-steel sink, and a microwave. There are two upper cabinets above the stove top and microwave and one lower cabinet under the sink. It's dinky, but efficient, and the water and electric are on. Past the kitchen is the bathroom. It's got a white pedestal sink, a rust stained but working toilet, and a tiled stall shower, also in working order. Across the hall are two bedrooms. One has a queen bed and a dresser and the other has two sets of bunkbeds with a chest of drawers in between. The furniture and mattresses are dingy but salvageable.

I release a heavy sigh. Cottage number four's repairs are all within my skillset. I can have it rentable and bringing in income in a couple of weeks. It'd be great if I can find a long-term renter like that Heather woman I met yesterday.

Moving on to cottage three, its layout is identical, but it has different issues. The wall around the woodstove chimney is black with soot and this room smells like a campfire, which is nice outdoors and problematic indoors. Unfortunately, the burnt aroma still lingers in the loveseat and armchair as well as the queen bed in the first bedroom. The bunkbed room doesn't stink, but the chest of drawers is missing the bottom drawer. In addition, there's a small hole, about the size of my fist, through the kitchen ceiling and roof, which let in rain in wetter times and warped the linoleum floor. However, bright side, the bathroom doesn't have any issues.

Cottages two and one... if I had the funds to hire a contractor, I would. In an attempt not to get discouraged, I add their myriad problems to my list and get out quickly. The only good thing I have to say about two and one are that I didn't see any evidence of rodents.

To get to cottages five through eight, I walk around by the residence, following the circular drive. The area in the middle of the circle still has waist high weeds, blackberry brambles, and kudzu overtaking the trees. If there are any rodents here, that's for sure their abode. No thanks!

The condition of the other four cottages is blessedly more like cottages three and four and less like two and one, with the exception that they all need new roofs. There is some heavy blue tarping going on.

After snarfing a peanut butter and strawberry jelly sandwich for lunch, I gather up my laptop and accoutrement and head to the Tyler Creek library.

The library is located near the high school and must have been built around the same time because both buildings are two story red brick blocks with centered banks of tall windows on the first and second floors.

I park in the newly repaved lot and enter the library through a wide set of glass and chrome double doors. Past the doors is a welcoming lobby with granite tiles floors and cream-colored walls hung with local artwork by both professionals and school kids. Three huge metal sculptural chandeliers hang from the ceiling. Public restrooms and drinking fountains are located on each side of another set of double doors leading into the library proper. There is a community meeting room situated at either end of the lobby.

I walk through the lower level that houses the children's books on the left, including a large, carpeted area outlined by colorful bean-bags that screams Storytime. To my right is the circulation and information desk and a dozen rows holding DVDs and CDs. In the center of the building are two staircases with four comfy couches between them, perfect for lounging and reading. I head up to the second level where in the center there are three rows of long worktables that have power outlets and USB ports built in.

Overstuffed chairs and couches are placed sporadically throughout the space. Along the edges of the second floor are the stacks containing fiction, non-fiction, periodicals, and a special room just for teens which appears to house tons of YA novels, manga, graphic novels, and a row of computers with a sign on the bright green wall above that says *Homework Club*.

Settling down into a low, overstuffed chair, I prop my feet up on an ottoman and fire up my computer. Then I access the website for the cottages that I began creating when I was still in Oregon.

Now that I've seen the property, the color scheme of light blues and greens I'd chosen still fits but the font is all wrong. It's more English countryside and less rustic cabin in the woods. I enjoy making custom websites – it's a weird way to unwind but I find the process... hopeful? Back in Braverton, I'd built Maryann's website for her store and Luis' for his restaurant, as well as Pinwheel Plant Shop's and, of course, the B&B.

Half an hour later, I've done everything I can do on the Enchanted site. What it really needs are loads of photos. Which can't come until after renovations, at least of cottage number four.

Thinking maybe I'll find a decent local business photographer on other Tyler Creek sites; I type in Tyler Creek Community Theatre. Their website is okay. Pretty basic and the photo credits are for Monica, so no luck there. I check out the Christmas shop which is not much more than pages and pages of stock.

It lacks personality. Not that I'll ever tell the owner that! There is a single picture of the shop that looks like it was taken from across Tyler's Way on someone's phone.

The cheese shop/café, Fromage, has great photography, but the pages are all black with white writing and my eyes strain to read the copy. I make note of the photographer's name and get off Fromage's website before I get a headache.

Dubois Photography has fantastic web design and when I scroll down to the bottom to see who made the website, the photographer Afton Dubois is listed. If times ever get tough in the photography biz, she can totally pivot to creating websites for other people.

Satisfied I've done all I can for now, I leave the library and drive over to the Kroger to pick-up apple pie ingredients, excited for another excuse to see Henry. The fact that he went out of his way for me, someone he hardly knows, touches my heart. Having him next door is reassuring. I hardly know him either, but I can already tell he's a good, solid guy. I want to get to know him better, which is something I haven't been able to say in a long time, not since before Nick disappeared in our brand-new RV, leaving me with debt up to my eyeballs and a healthy skepticism when it came to men and their intentions.

But I'm getting ahead of myself. I'm baking Henry a pie, not offering him a piece of my heart.

Seven

Henry

The phone on the kitchen wall rings as I'm on my way out the door. I almost don't answer it, but I double-back and pick up in case it's Lettie. No sense in telling her she can call me if she needs me and then not follow through.

"Hello?"

"Henry? It's Lettie." She's whispering into the phone, her voice trembling.

The hairs on the back of my neck stand up.

"Everything okay, neighbor?" I ask, attempting to calm her by using an even, relaxed voice. The one I use when the horses get skittish.

Lettie squeaks out a nervous laugh. "Oh, I don't know. It's probably nothing but…"

My shoulders tense. "But what?"

"I think someone's watching me."

"You what now?" I pace the length of the kitchen and back twisting the long curly cord around and around my forearm.

"I can sense someone's eyes on me," Lettie says. "You know that spooked feeling?" She laughs again. "Do I sound crazy? I must sound crazy to you."

I wrack my brain for any news of recent break ins or suspicious folks around Tyler Creek. I like to listen to the police scanner to pass the time during chores, with police permission, of course. Nothing comes to mind.

"You don't sound crazy, you sound rattled," I say, shaking the phone cord loose from my arm. "Want me to come by and check things out real quick?"

She lets out a breath. "Would you? I'd sure appreciate it. Although, it sounds like you're in a hurry."

"I've got the time to help," I say.

"Oh, good. To make the hassle more enticing, I've made you two apple pies to thank you for all the work you did clearing the driveway."

I grin. She wasn't kidding about getting right to the baking. "It's no hassle. I'll be over in a minute."

"Thank you," she says, relief in her voice.

We hang up, and I jog out to my pickup. My mouth waters at the prospect of apple pie, which I don't have time for this evening, but as my granny used to say, anticipation is one of life's greatest pleasures.

I'm at Lettie's in about three minutes, parking the truck in front of the first cottage. I grab a flashlight from the space behind my seat. Like I said, my phone is old. So old it doesn't have a flashlight on it and the photo quality is grainy at best. I prefer to take photos with my nice digital camera, anyway, but it does tend to confuse people that I only use my cell phone as a phone.

I stand still in the middle of the drive, listening. The light's dimmer here than at my place, which is out in the open away from these woods. I can see how easy it would be to freak yourself out if you're not used to the sounds of nature.

Rustling comes from the mess of weeds and vines and kudzu in the center circle of the drive. I approach the area, my flashlight on but pointed at the ground. I'm not afraid of critters, really, although I'd like to avoid stirring up a rat's nest if possible. Scary? No. Gross? Yep.

My boots scrape lightly against the gravel road as I peer into the dark green chaos before me.

A hiss emanates from the weeds, and I spot the foliage swaying in several places.

Whatever it is, there's more than one.

Slowly, I raise the flashlight, the glare reflecting off of about a dozen pairs of eyes staring back at me.

I stamp my foot, sending the animals scattering in all directions, including mine.

"Oh, boy," I say, chuckling. Well, at least there's nothing for her to be afraid of.

I stride to the house and up the front steps, a smile on my face. Lettie opens the door before I get a chance to knock.

"Is there something out there?" she asks, waving me into the house.

I stay put and nod toward the weedy circle. "Come see for yourself. Put your mind at ease."

When she hesitates, I offer her my hand and she takes it. Her fingers are hot, her palm a little sweaty, but the contact is nice. I can't remember the last time I held a woman's hand like this, not in service of helping them off a horse.

She lets me lead her down the stairs and over to the center of the circle.

"Look here," I say, shining the flashlight into the grass again.

Lettie grips my hand harder. "What am I looking at?"

I glance at her, and she's got her eyes nearly closed. She sure is cute.

"That would be a whole mess of feral cats."

Lettie opens her eyes wide and let's go of my hand, dropping down to get a better look. "Here kitty, kitty," she beckons.

"They're wild," I say.

She rolls her eyes at me. "I know what feral means."

I smirk. "Okay, but you're calling them like they're housecats."

Lettie shrugs and stands up. "I'll bet they'll come to me if I offer them some food."

I gently grab her by the arm when she moves to head back to the house. "Don't feed them people food. I'm sure they're getting enough to eat what with all the rodents that must be out here."

Lettie considers this. "I haven't seen a single rat or mouse yet." She steps closer to the weeds. "Thanks kitties." Lettie raises an eyebrow at me. "This mean man won't let me feed you turkey lunch meat, just so you know. It's not me it's him."

An absolute knock-out smile spreads across her lips and I can't help but smile back at her. "I don't guess I've ever had anyone throw me under the bus to a pack of feral cats before."

She snorts a laugh. "What do you think? Should we cohabitate?"

A thrill shoots through my chest before I realize she's talking about the cats. *Get a grip, Hank.*

"My advice would be to keep two, so the rodent population stays down and have animal control come get the rest of the cats."

Lettie nods. "You think two is enough?

What if they have a rat attack plan that only works if they all band together and use their specific skills to vanquish their enemy?"

I tip my head side-to-side. "Well, now, I hadn't considered that they may have a coordinated strategy… mostly because if they did, they would've taken over the world by now, don't you think?"

"Fine," Lettie says and sighs. She chucks me on the arm. "I've wrapped up the pies to-go, but why don't I cut us both a piece? Who knows how long we have before our feline overlords get wise." She grins. "I've got vanilla ice cream to go with it."

I look at my wristwatch. "I'd love nothing more than to have a slice of pie with you, Lettie, but I've got to head to the Tyler Creek Small Business Association meeting. I'm giving a presentation on customer retention. We meet twice a month. You'll have to come to the next one. If I wasn't speaking tonight, I'd bail."

She waves her invitation away. "Raincheck?"

I nod. "Raincheck."

Lettie turns toward the house. "I'll go fetch the pies."

I grasp her arm to stop her again. "Why don't you keep them here. It'll give me a good excuse to visit you soon."

I suppose what I've just said sounds okay because her eyes light up when I say I'll visit soon.

"No excuse needed to drop in, neighbor," Lettie says. She pats my hand on her arm. "Thanks for coming to my rescue again."

"It's not a problem." I tip my hat to her.

"I'll walk you to your truck," she says. "So we don't say goodbye and then awkwardly walk in the same direction. I hate that when it happens."

I chuckle. "Me too. I feel the need to say bye, like, six times."

We get to my truck, and I open the door. "Bye, Lettie. See you soon."

"Bye, Henry." She doesn't make to back away from the truck. Her eyes are bright with mischief.

Oh, I get it. "So long, Lettie."

"Au revoir, Henry."

"Later, Lettie-gator."

She snorts a laugh and then composes herself. "After while, Henry-dile."

With that, Lettie turns and strides back to her house.

Customer retention seems way less important than Lettie retention at this moment, but I get in my truck and go, coming up with a plan for tomorrow. Because no way am I waiting longer than that before I see her again.

Eight

Henry

"Yep. That sounds real bad," I say into the phone after Bobby, the head of my noonday private trail ride group, shares that he and his entire family have all come down with a nasty stomach bug.

Normally I wouldn't be thankful for a last-minute cancelation, but now my afternoon is free, and I can pay Lettie a visit earlier than I'd planned.

"I'll reimburse you less the hundred-dollar reservation fee. No problem."

"Thanks, Henry," Bobby says. "Um, I gotta go. Sorry!" He ends the call. I imagine to go find the nearest restroom.

Happy not to have a stomach bug, I put my black hat on and step out onto my front porch. It's a gorgeous day. Little hot, but the humidity is bearable, and the sky is that cloudless muted robin's egg blue of mid-summer.

I decide to walk over to Lettie's, along the road. It'd technically be shorter to go through the woods, but I'd have to hack my way through, and I don't want to be showing up all pitted out and stinking.

No one drives past as I walk, so the only thing kicking up dust is my boots. The scent of gardenia and honeysuckle floats on the air. I reckon the gardenia aroma is coming from Afton Dubois' place up the road past Lettie's and across the way. She's got a bunch of them encircling her house. The honeysuckle is nearer, tangled up in the woods I didn't get to the other day.

I'm about halfway down Lettie's drive, grateful for the shady reprieve from the beating sun, when I realize I probably should've called her to see if she was home.

But I'm almost there and the walking is nice… and I left my phone behind charging in my office anyhow.

"Arrrrrggggghhhh!" I hear Lettie yell.

I pick up my pace, although that was definitely more of a *I'm about to kick this here thing* yell than one of danger.

Sure enough, as I round the bend, I spot Lettie gesticulating at something on the ground next to the third cottage. And then she kicks it, hurts her foot, and limps toward the porch steps where she sits down.

She's got her head in her hands and a shake in her shoulders that looks like she's crying. That won't do at all.

"Everything all right, neighbor?" I holler to her.

She looks up, wipes her eyes and gives me a sheepish smile.

"Do you have a shotgun, because I'd really like to shoot this good-for-nothing gutter to pieces."

"Nope, sorry. Just a bb gun to scare off coyotes."

"Darn. I don't suppose coyotes eat gutters." She stands up, puts weight on her foot, shakes it out and then walks to me. "Apple pie will probably make things better, don't you think?"

"Always." I glance at the busted gutter as I pass by. It's rusty and full of mud and moss. "I suspect that gutter is a loss."

Lettie sighs. "I know, but I'm trying to cut corners wherever I can. I don't have enough money yet to fix all the cottages up like they require and since I had no idea things were this bad, it's going to be awhile."

My first inclination is to offer to help her with the stuff I know I can easily do, like hang a gutter, but I don't want her to think I don't think she's capable. I'm certain she's just as capable as I am, at least.

So, I nod in commiseration. "I get it. If buildings aren't maintained, then they can go downhill real quick. I'm forever replacing stuff on my barn."

She trudges up the porch steps. "It's just that... I'm not *not* handy. A gutter shouldn't defeat me."

I shrug. "Oh, well, maybe the next one won't."

"Yeah," she says. "I can only hope. Or move on to something less frustrating like re-finishing wood floors."

Shoot, I don't have a clue how to do that. She'll probably end up helping me with D.I.Y. in the long run.

I follow her inside the house, a rush of childhood memories flooding my brain.

"This place is like a time-capsule," I say, scanning the front room. "Looks the same as it did when I was a kid. Is that old table from Wendy's still here?"

Lettie throws a grin over her shoulder. "It is." She crooks her finger at me as she walks into the kitchen. "Why don't you pour us a couple glasses of iced tea and I'll get the pie."

"Will do." I find six plain glasses next to six white cereal bowls and six white plates in the most logical cabinet.

"My best friend back home, Maryann, would be appalled at my Dollar Tree dishes." She chuckles. "I'll get something cute when these cottages are turning a profit."

I shrug and pull the clear plastic pitcher of tea out of the fridge. "I inherited the house I grew up in and the dishes that came with it when my folks moved to Florida." Furrowing my brow, I try to recall what brand the dishes are. "They're yellow and orange... *Fiestaware*."

"Nice," Lettie says, expertly removing a slice of pie from an aluminum pie pan. "An American classic. Some people collect Fiestaware, even."

I return the pitcher to the fridge and take the tea over to the table. "Huh. Well, I just eat off of them."

Lettie brings the pie and ice cream over on the too-big dinner plates with a fork nestled on top and sets one in front of me. She sits down opposite. "Do you collect anything? I collect salt and pepper shakers, but they're in a box in the hall closet for now until I figure out where to display them."

"I do," I say, my cheeks heating. I jam a big ol' bite of pie in my mouth, stalling. Only Mom and Granny know about my collection. "Mmm mmm, this is some delicious nostalgia right here."

"Our family recipe is the best, I gotta say." She rolls her lips together. "Wanna know what the secret ingredient is?"

I take a gulp of my tea. "Of course."

"First you have to tell me what you collect. I know you thought I was gonna let that slide." She giggles.

I roll my eyes at her. "It's not so much that

I'm embarrassed, but it's weird for someone our age to be into this."

Lettie waves my words away. "Please. People like what they like."

"I sure do like this pie," I say, taking another bite, this time with a helping of vanilla ice cream.

"Uh huh." She sips her tea and waits for me to finish chewing, her dark blue eyes fixed on me.

What man can resist a look like that? And why would he want to? "All right, all right. I collect souvenir bells."

She raises her eyebrows. "Like the little white ceramic ones you can get at truck stops?"

"Yeah, although I've got some metal ones too. And they don't only come from truck stops. I've found a lot of mine at swap meets and flea markets. My granny got me started on them when she took me on a trip to Nashville to visit her cousin. That one's got a guitar on it."

Lettie forks a bite of pie and swirls it in melted ice cream before bringing it to her smiling lips. "I didn't expect tiny bells, Henry. That *is* a unique collection for someone our age."

I smirk. "Unique, huh? You just think I'm weird." Lettie wouldn't be the first to think that. Likely why I get along better with horses than most women.

She chuckles and takes a swig of tea. "I've got a salt and pepper shaker from the sixties that's a muscle man flexing, and the S and P are his pumped-up biceps. How's that for weird?"

"These salt and pepper shakers aren't functional, are they?"

"They're art. Like your wee tinkly bells." She winks at me and I almost choke.

When I can breathe again, I point at my last bite of pie with my fork. "What's the secret ingredient?"

Lettie finishes off her piece. "A quarter cup of sweet pickle juice."

I savor my final bite, trying to ascertain a pickle-ish flavor.

She shakes her head. "The vinegar somehow makes the apples more apple-y. You won't taste pickle."

"You're right, I don't."

Lettie takes our plates over to the sink and runs water on them to soak. "It just occurred to me that you're here in the middle of the day. Is it your day off?"

"Had a cancelation. I was gonna come over and see you anyway." We smile at each other and my cheeks heat. What is with this woman and all the blushing she's making me do? "I thought maybe you'd like to take a ride with me."

She leans a hip against the counter. "Like in your truck?"

I chuckle and stand, handing her her glass of tea from the table. "Like on a horse." Her eyes go wide. "If you want to. I know you have gutters to murder and whatnot."

Lettie finishes her tea and nods, deciding. "Horseback riding sounds like a more fun thing to fail at."

I come around the counter and set my empty glass in the sink next to the plates, our arms brushing against one another. "I'll bet you're a natural and if not, I won't let you fail."

She tilts her head, studying me. "You know what, Henry? I believe you."

I don't even want to know how pink my face is right now.

Nine

Lettie

We walk to Henry's place in companionable silence, both of us turning our faces up to the clear blue sky every now and then. Our trip from mine to his only takes about ten minutes on foot. No wonder he's been so quick to my rescue.

Past the mailbox, the gravel driveway goes up a little hill and then over that straight on to the house. To the left of the drive is a gravel parking area outlined with railroad ties and backed by a landscaped yard with six white picnic tables and the same number of old wine barrel planters overflowing with red and white impatiens and purple wave petunias. Beyond that are stables, a corral, and a pasture which backs up to the woods between our properties.

On the opposite side of the driveway there is a grassy lawn broken up with three groups of enormous blue hydrangeas – the plants are so huge and established, it's hard to tell exactly how many there are. The two-story farmhouse is painted a crisp white with dark green shutters and front door. A welcoming porch, with five baskets dripping with red flowers hanging every few feet from the ceiling along the front, wraps around to the right side. I can spot the corner of a fenced in veggie garden near the back of the house. From a metal archway hangs some type of green bean and the silky tassels of corn are visible.

"Henry, your property is gorgeous," I say, smiling at him as we walk the path to the stables. "It's so inviting. You do all of this yourself?"

He ducks his head. "Thank you. My parents are responsible for the look of the house and the private yard. I did put in the parking lot and picnic area." He gives me a crooked smile. "The first step in customer retention at Tyler Creek Trail Rides is plenty of room for people to park their vehicles and have a leisurely lunch."

"What's step two?" I ask, following him into the tidy and only slightly smelly wood building.

"Offering a variety of trail rides for every level of rider and switching them up from season to season." Henry stops at a room to our right which is across from the beginning of a row of stalls. The neat hand painted sign above the doorway says Tack Room in shiny black. He turns to me, giving me an assessing look.

I blush under his gaze and become interested in the brown horse with its head jutting over the metal gate of the first stall. It sort of looks me over too and then snorts.

Henry laughs. "That's Jasper. He's a persnickety old man. I usually put big guys on him." Henry dips into the tack room and returns with a saddle and a blanket and the strappy bridle thingy. "This one should be the most comfortable for you. I'll put you on

Winnie. She's a sweetheart." He grins. "Only a lil bit persnickety."

"A girl after my own heart. I like her already." I hold out my hands to take some of the gear from him, but he winks at me.

"I got it."

Henry leads me down the concrete walkway between a dozen stalls – eight on the left, and four on the right just after the tack room and a small office. He nudges the latch on the gate up with his elbow. "Hey, Winnie girl. This here's Lettie. You be on your best behavior."

Winnie, who'd had her face down in a feeding trough of some sort, lifts her head up and rambles over to Henry.

"I'll get her tacked up," Henry says over his shoulder. "You can watch from there and then I'll let you give it a go next time."

I nod and lean against the gate all nonchalant, like he didn't just insinuate going for rides would be a regular occurrence.

Henry moves with efficient grace, murmuring sweet words to Winnie while he's tacking her up and making adjustments. I attempt to concentrate on what he's doing; I imagine this is a good skill to add to one's arsenal, but I maybe get a tiny bit mesmerized with watching Henry's face more than his hands. Not that his hands aren't all strong and rugged and nice to look at too.

When he's finished, Henry turns to me and hands me the reins.

"Go ahead and lead her out of the stall."

Panic shoots through me for a second before Winnie simply walks out of the stall without me really having to do anything. She stops in the aisle, so I stop in the aisle.

"I'm gonna go fetch my horse, Edgar, and meet you back here in a sec."

Edgar's stall is all the way at the end, but he's already got all his stuff on, so Winnie and I aren't waiting long.

"Alrighty, let's get you out to the steps and onto Winnie," Henry says, clicking his tongue, signaling the horses, and me too I guess, to follow.

We exit out the far end of the stables opposite the tack room and walk to a set of four steps with a small platform. Henry takes Winnie's reins from me and nods for me to go up the steps as Winnie gets into place.

"Get a good grip on the saddle horn with

your left hand and put your left foot into the stirrup," Henry instructs.

With absolutely zero grace, I do as he tells me.

"Now, hop on your right foot and swing your leg up and over Winnie."

I give him a look that says easier said than done, but then I hop and swing my leg over Winnie and it's pretty easy. I pat Winnie on the neck. "Thanks for staying still, girl."

Henry helps me get my tennis shoe into the stirrup.

"Feel comfortable? Your foot should be in but have the ability to slide out easily."

I wiggle both feet like I know what sensation I'm testing, but it all seems... fine?

"I'm good, I think."

Henry nods and then mounts Edgar in, like, five seconds straight off the ground.

"Show off," I say.

He rolls his eyes. "I've only been doing this since I was three years old."

"So, thirty years?" I ask. I know Henry's younger than I am, but not by how much.

"Smooth," he says, shaking his head at me. "I'm forty, Lettie. Been riding for thirty-seven years."

"I'll be forty-five in September," I offer.

"I know," says Henry.

I raise an eyebrow at him.

"Well, I knew you were fiveish years older, not when your birthday is." He grins. "I remember being nervous about riding ponies with you back in the day. You were almost a teenager!"

I laugh. "Practically ancient. And then I was insufferable and refused to ride with you. What a jerk pre-teen Lettie was."

"Aw, let's forgive her," Henry says, giving Edgar a tap on the side with the heel of his boot. Our horses start to walk. "Everyone is insufferable when they're twelve."

"I'll bet you weren't," I say, holding onto the saddle horn in a desperate attempt not to slip off Winnie's undulating back. "You seemed like the sort of kid who was more comfortable around grown-ups."

"Heh," Henry says. "You got me."

Winnie falls in line behind Edgar as we head to the trail at the edge of the property near the road.

"Where to?" I ask, settling in by shifting my weight back and down into the saddle.

"I thought we'd take the trail by Tyler Creek," he says. "It's not too long, about an hour. I don't want you to be too sore what with all the D.I.Y. you've got ahead of you."

"Let's not speak of that right now," I say, chuckling.

Henry turns in the saddle and mimes zipping his lips.

We meander down the trail, the same one Henry was on when we first met. I've seen him every day since and it doesn't feel like too much. I've never minded being alone, which has been a problem in relationships in the past, but maybe I just hadn't met a man I wanted to see every day?

Good grief, Leticia Marie Montague, get a hold of yourself! It's been four days.

I shake my head and smile to myself; glad Henry's back is to me because according to Maryann my facial expressions give everything I'm thinking away.

I take in my surroundings. There's a stillness here. The fields we pass by are a patchwork of golden sun-dried grasses and purple, yellow, pink, and blue wildflowers floating above green foliage. The breeze and birds are taking an afternoon nap, the only sounds are the clip-clop of our horse's hooves and the slap of my ankles against Winnie's sides.

We turn left onto a red dirt trail that skirts the edges of someone's peach orchard before disappearing into dense shaded woods. The trail's entrance is marked by a wooden sign with an arrow, underneath a towering, gnarled oak tree to one side. I recognize it as one of my landmarks – *big ol twisty tree*. We're still fairly close to home.

"Is this trail only for your horses or could I use it for walking?" I ask. For the sake of my mental health and the size of my rear end, I need to get back into a daily walking habit.

"It's a public trail for anyone to use. All the ones around here are. They're maintained by Tyler Creek Park and Recreation." He jabs a thumb behind him. "Did you see the sign back there under the tree?"

"The one with the arrow?"

"Yeah. The name of the trail is on the sign too, but hard to read from up here. We're on Creek Trail right now."

"I'm assuming because it leads to Tyler Creek?" I joke.

Henry shakes his head. "Nah, the family that owns the orchard's last name is Creek."

"Really? That's serendipitous."

He twists toward me, a wide smile on his face. "No, not really. I'm pulling your leg."

I stick my tongue out at him. "Rude." I shrug. "In Braverton, most things are named after old white dudes, so Creek as a last name is plausible."

We enter the shade of the woods, and the temperature blessedly drops ten degrees.

"Tell me about Oregon," Henry says, absently stroking Edgar's mane.

"Is this interest as a peace offering for teasing me or do you actually want to know?"

He looks back at me, his eyebrows knit together in seriousness. "I actually want to know."

"You've never been?" I ask.

Henry shakes his head. "Nope. Never made it out to Oregon or Washington."

"Oregon is beautiful in many of the same ways it is here. Rolling hills and mountains. Abundant rivers and creeks. Greener, though, at least in the Tualatin Valley where I come from."

"Because of all the rain?" Edgar pauses, rips a clump of grass from the side of the trail with his mouth and resumes walking.

"Yeah. It rains most of the year, but then not at all in the summer." It had been a hundred degrees every day the week I left. Despite all the rain, Oregon was always on the cusp of drought.

"Huh. Summer without big thunderstorms? Weird." He chuckles.

I look around, even through the trees the sun shines bright. "I can't picture that. I haven't seen many clouds but those wispy ones since I got here."

"Oh, the storms sneak up on us. They usually roll in, cause a ruckus, and then roll out within a few hours."

"Thunder bolts and lightning?"

"Very, very fright-ning," Henry sings.

I grin at him even though he isn't facing me. "Really?"

"Nah. I actually like 'em. Nature's catharsis."

Winnie stops and bends her head, chewing at the grass. Unlike Edgar, she doesn't keep moving.

"Um… help?" I ask.

Henry glances back. "C'mon Winnie girl."

She slowly raises her head and plods along again.

"What about tornadoes?" I ask, picking our conversation up. "They exist in Oregon, but they're usually not too destructive."

He nods. "We have a few warnings in the springtime. A proper tornado hasn't blown through Tyler Creek since the late nineties."

Phew. "I'll admit I was sort of worried about them. Fear of the unknown and all that."

He nods. "I get it. I'm irrationally afraid of earthquakes and I'll bet you've been in a bunch of those."

"Not as often as in California, but yeah, at least once every couple of years there will be a mild one. I definitely won't miss the threat of the big one that could hit at any time." I'd heard on NPR that seismologists were concerned it was going to be apocalyptic.

"What do you miss about Oregon?" Henry asks.

I consider his question and a pang of guilt hits me. "Honestly, I only really miss Maryann and her husband, Luis. Everyone in Braverton is lovely, and the town is comfortable and familiar, but I don't long for them or it... yet. Ask me again when I'm knee deep in renovations, crying into my fifteenth bent gutter."

Henry chuckles. "Your folks still there? In Braverton?"

"No, they live in Kauai now. Although, even when they lived in Braverton I didn't see them that often. They're older and I'm an only child. They retired when I was in my late twenties."

"Yep. I know how that goes. My parents are older too."

"People always think my dad is my grandpa." I laugh. "He isn't the type to care about such things, though."

"Maybe it has less to do with him and more to do with your youthful appearance?" Henry asks.

"I doubt that. He's got gray hair and tons of wrinkles, and I would too if it wasn't for hair dye and moisturizer."

Henry points to his hat. "We'll get you one of these to help keep the sun off."

"Is that the secret to your babyface?"

"Ha." He shrugs. "Well, I gotta keep my

face lookin' good to distract from the fact the rodeo took its toll on my body."

What now? "You were in the rodeo? Like a bull rider?"

He nods. "I started out with bull riding, but saddle bronc riding is what I was known for."

"Known for? Are you a famous cowboy, Henry?"

Henry shrugs again. "Used to be. But that was a while ago."

"You know the instant I get my internet set up I'm going to Google you and saddle bronc riding."

"Google away. I don't mind."

A gentle breeze kicks up, cooling the back of my neck, and sending the fragrance of honeysuckle my way. I can hear the faint sounds of rushing water up ahead. Tyler Creek must be close.

The trail splits off to the right, marked with another sign pointing toward the Enchanted Caverns. We continue on down the Creek Trail.

"You know I've never even been to the caverns my cottages are named after?" I ask.

"I think Aunt Lettie tried to take me, but y'-know, *twelve*."

"That'll have to be our next ride then."

There Henry goes again with promises of future adventures.

"You know the story of their supposed enchantment?" he asks, bringing me back to the present.

I flip through the packet of documents the lawyer sent in my mind. "Something about if you go there with your sweetheart and your love is true, the caverns will gift you all with a happy life together?"

"That's the gist," he says.

"What do you think? Is it true?" I ask.

He tilts his head from side to side. "I don't know as it really matters if it's true or not. People do like their romantic notions."

I think about the boxes of paperback romances I'd donated to Maryann's shop before I moved out here. A lot of them had a cowboy love interest. *Huh.* "They certainly do."

As if he knows what I'm thinking without even looking at my face full of tells, Henry turns to me. "I don't mind."

My cheeks heat as he holds my gaze for a

moment before clearing his throat. "The creek is just around the next bend."

"Fantastic. I love a good creek." My blush blushes.

"We'll dismount the horses there." He smirks, not unkindly. "Stick our toes in the water. Cool down some."

* * *

Ten minutes later, we emerge from the woods onto a narrow, rocky beach. Tyler Creek is almost wide enough to be considered a river, but shallow enough rocks jut out of the water all the way across.

Henry gets off of Edgar in a flash and then he's next to me, offering me a hand down. I'm about as graceful getting off of Winnie as I was getting on, which is to say not very, but at least I don't faceplant.

The horses stick to the shade under the trees while Henry and I shuck off our shoes and roll up our pants legs.

"See that flat rock there?" he asks, pointing about ten feet from shore. "That's where we're headed. I'll go first. Step where I step."

I do as he says, and we make it out to the rock without incident.

"Remember 'laying out'?" I ask after we take a seat side-by-side.

He raises an eyebrow.

"You know, sunbathing. It was popular when we were kids and teenagers, but nowadays people know to avoid getting sunburnt."

"Must have been a female thing," he says. "What of it?"

I lean back on my hands, lifting my face to the sky. "This rock is perfect for it. Back in the day I would've plopped myself here for hours with my Walk-Man, a two-liter of Diet Rite, and few copies of Sassy or Seventeen magazine."

He chuckles, dipping a cupped hand into the chilly water and letting it run through his fingers. "Like a turtle, sunning itself on a rock. I get ya."

I close my eyes to the sun and let its warmth sink into me. "Exactly like a turtle. Only with way more responsibilities. Even back then."

"Oh?" he asks.

"Nothing too deep," I say, opening my eyes and smiling at him. "Just homework and chores and babysitting to earn enough money to blow on tapes at Tower Records."

"We didn't have anything near as fancy as a Tower Records," Henry says, "but there used to be a music store on Tyler's Way. Mike's Music and Other Cool Stuff."

"Not the easiest name to fit on an awning." Of course, Maryann's shop is called the Secondhand Rose Vintage Thrift Shop. What a mouthful!

Henry nods. "The best part is the guy who owned the place was called Tom. I don't know who Mike was."

"Quintessential small town. I love it," I say, paddling my feet, sticking them up out of the water. They're getting a little numb.

"Are you going to keep the name Enchanted Cavern Cottages?" he asks, lifting his feet out of the water as well.

I shrug. "I think so. I mean, I've already got a sign."

"A half-rotted sign."

"True, but of all the things I have to do, fixing up the sign is going to be easy peasy."

"About that," Henry says, sliding a glance my way. "If you need some help, don't hesitate to ask. I don't mind. Even if it's just finishing hacking up the weeds and carting them away. It's too much work for one person."

Tears threaten to well in my eyes, but I blink them away, shoving down the overwhelm of what lies ahead of me. "That's sweet of you, Henry, but we haven't known each other for long and what you're proposing is more than neighborly obligation. Besides, you must have plenty of work to keep you busy."

He nods. "I do, but like I said before, my folks had systems in place that made it easy to take things over from them. You got a raw deal, and it wouldn't be right for me to sit by and watch you struggle without lending a hand. However long we've known each other or not."

Why in the world am I resistant to his offer? This is a dumb time for me to acquire pride. I nod back at him. "Okay. I would appreciate your help, but if it keeps you from getting your own work done, promise me you'll make your business your priority."

"Sounds like a plan." He wets his fingertips and flicks the water away. "Ready to head back and beat some gutters into submission?"

I shake my head in mock solemnity. "Poor

gutters, what did they ever do to warrant all this violence from us?"

He chuckles. "Well, I guess I could've said lovingly coax them into behaving." Henry mimes petting something, presumably a gutter.

This man. "Yes, I guess you could've."

Ten

Henry

Three days after our ride, I drive past a white Animal Control van with its back door open revealing several traps stacked on top of one another and park my truck next to Lettie's car alongside her house.

We'd spent the late afternoon and evening the day before clearing out the weeds and brambles and vines in the middle of the circular drive to make it easier to find the cats.

Lettie's got her arms crossed and is nodding her head. As of last night, she still hadn't decided which two cats she was going to keep.

I stroll over, nodding to the animal control officer who'd come from Bentonville as Tyler Creek doesn't have one of their own.

"Howdy," I say. "Thanks for coming out." The man and I do a quick handshake.

"Maybe you can talk some sense into your girlfriend." He heads toward the back of his van.

I turn to Lettie. We both let the girlfriend thing slide without correcting him. Her eyes are red rimmed like she's been crying. *Well, that won't do.*

"What's the matter?" I ask, reaching out and patting her on the arm. "Having a hard time deciding which two are staying?"

She shakes her head and glares in the officer's direction. "They euthanize them. Bentonville doesn't have a trap, neuter, release program like practically every other animal control in the country."

"Shoot," I say. We'd expected that the cats would be fixed and immunized and... well, we didn't know where they'd be released, but we figured there was a known place for that sort of thing.

"Did you ask about him trapping the two for us to take to the vet?"

She nods. "Officer Reinhardt here said he'd do that for a hundred dollars per cat."

"Ouch." We'd assumed that would be free of charge. It appears the ten-minute internet search Lettie did on feral cat control at the library was misleading. I should've known better.

"The only thing that's free is him trapping them and hauling them back to Bentonville to be put to death!"

The officer rolls his eyes at me as if to say *Women, huh?* "They're humanely euthanized, Ms. Montague." He walks over to the edge of the circle, where the grass is still tall, so we didn't drive the cats away, and sets down two traps. "They're feral cats, not endangered baby seals."

"What do you want to do?" I ask, keeping my voice low so Officer Jerk Face can't interject anymore of his less than helpful comments. "You can't afford to pay for him to trap them all can you? Plus, the vet bill to neuter and immunize a dozen cats isn't going to be cheap."

Lettie's shoulders slump and she screws

her eyes shut for a moment, thinking, or fretting or wishing she'd never come to Tyler Creek. I hope it's not the last one.

"I can't let the cats get killed and I can't not get them fixed or I'll end up with forty by next summer." She opens her eyes and looks at the circle as Officer Reinhardt sets two more traps down.

"So, what am I doing?" he asks. "Trapping two, trapping them all…"

Lettie puts her hands on her hips. "Trap them all and if it's not too much trouble, can you take them to Tyler Creek Veterinary Clinic?"

"For a fee, 'course I can."

"You sure?" I ask her. "I can help with the vet bill. Maybe Doctor Charlie will give you a group discount or something since he's been treating my horses for as long as I can remember."

Lettie's eyes soften. "You're already going above and beyond, Henry. I'll just… advertise that the Enchanted Cavern Cottages has a cat sanctuary or something. Surely, that sort of thing is a tax write off."

My hand twitches with the urge to tuck a

lock of hair that's come free of her ponytail behind her ear. Instead…

"Is this your way of getting out of having to choose two?" I joke.

She snorts and tucks the lock herself. "You've got my number."

Officer Reinhardt strides over with a clipboard in one hand, an ink pen in the other. "Paperwork and payment first and then you're the proud owner of a dozen mangy feral cats. Congratulations."

"Thanks," Lettie says, taking, well, yanking, the clipboard and pen from his hands.

The officer gives a smug chuckle. "Cash, check, or card?"

"Debit card," Lettie says, not looking up from the form.

"Okay, let me get my phone card reader doohickey from the van."

After the form is filled out and the payment is processed – for which we all had to walk clear to the road to get the reader to work – Lettie and I leave the officer to it and go into cottage four to paint the interior. Lettie had managed to strike a deal with Duncan over at the hardware store since she'd bought four five-gallon buckets of off-white paint with the promise of buying at least four more.

"We're going to be dreaming in off-white for weeks," I say, picking up a roller attached to a long pole and dipping it into the paint tray.

Lettie grins, twisting her roller onto another long pole. "Oh, I almost forgot. I picked up a CD player. Want to listen to some tunes?"

I put my roller to the left side front room wall. "Sure do. It'll make the work go faster."

She lays her roller down and zips over to her house, retrieving the CD player.

"I hope you like Janis Joplin," she says, plugging the boom box into a wall socket.

"Love, Janis," I say, getting more paint on my roller.

Lettie shakes her head. "For some reason I expected you to only like country music."

I wink at her, and she blushes. I'm a little bit addicted to making Lettie blush. "Is it because of the hat?" I tease.

"And the boots. And the truck. And the horses. All you're missing is a dog." She lifts the lid of the player and drops a CD in.

"I'm more of a dozen feral cats kinda guy," I say.

She mimics wiping sweat from her brow. "Phew!"

As the opening notes of *Me and Bobby McGee* play, Lettie retrieves her roller, singing into it like it's a microphone.

This woman.

"You've got a great voice," I say. "If being the proprietor of vacation cottages and a cat sanctuary falls through, you should start a Janis cover band."

Lettie twirls the roller and then dips it into the tray. "Lettie and the Piece of My Hearts?"

Take it!

"Already your Plan B?"

She laughs and paints a big M in the center of the opposing wall. "The cover band was Plan A." She nods to the wall. "This is my Plan B."

I turn back to my wall. "Have mercy."

Eleven

Lettie

"I told him that I could kiss him, and young Mr. Internet Installer Guy looked at me like I was a creepy old lady," I tell Maryann via Facetime.

She bursts out laughing. "Perhaps you should retire that phrase or only use it on your hot cowboy," Maryann says.

I look around the front room of my house like Henry is going to pop up out of nowhere and make fun of me for liking him.

"What is that you're sitting on?" Maryann asks, leaning closer to her computer screen.

I stand up and aim my web cam down to let her get a better look at the kitchen chair I've been dragging back and forth the past two days. "Obviously, I need to do some furniture shopping. I'm still sleeping on the old mattress covered in sleeping bags, too."

Maryann wrinkles her nose. "Gross. I can't believe I'm saying this but is there an Ikea anywhere nearby?"

Flopping back into the chair, it's my turn to burst out laughing. "Hours away." I think for a minute. "I'm not sure there's even one in this state."

"You're too old to be living like a college kid. People our age require orthopedic and ergonomic."

"My back agrees, but my bank account... it is what it is. All my funds need to go to renovations so that I can eventually make my bajillions." I chuckle. "There's a discount furniture store in town that I'll make it to one of these days.

"That's the pits, Let." Maryann frowns. "And I won't tell you that you shouldn't have kept all those cats because, obvs, you had to. I just wish you didn't have to deal with all this alone."

I shrug. "I'm not, really. Henry is being so helpful. In fact, he's picking the wild kitty gang up from the vet this afternoon."

"Bless his heart," Maryann says. "Did I use that expression right?"

"Around these here parts," I say, putting on my best twangy accent, "it's kind of condescending, but I get what you mean."

Luis comes into the frame and waves at me over Maryann's shoulder. "Hola, Leticia."

"Hola, Luis."

Maryann's husband drops a kiss onto the top of her head. "Lunch is ready, mi amor."

"I'll let you go," I say. "I need to go check if the mortar around the woodstove in cottage four is dry."

"What did we ever do before YouTube D.I.Y. videos?"

"We languished in blissful ignorance." I make a kissy face at my best friend. "Love you, talk soon."

"Love you," Maryann says and then ends the call.

Two hours later, Henry finds me in cottage four touching up the paint in the hallway.

It's really coming along. All that's left is flooring and furniture.

"Want to help me release the cats?" he asks, removing his hat and swiping a knuckle across his damp brow. There are scratches on the back of his hand.

I cringe. "Let me guess, herding cats is like herding cats?"

Henry puts his hat on. "Bingo. It took me, Doctor Charlie, and two vet techs, both named Sheila, to get the cats into their cardboard carriers and onto the truck. Thankfully, releasing them should be less dangerous."

I set my paintbrush down in the paint tray and follow him outside to where his truck is parked.

Absolute screeching cacophony fills the truck bed, as does the smell of pee.

"I'll get your truck detailed," I say. "This is nasty."

He shrugs. "I'll just hose 'er down, no biggie."

Henry lowers the gate and I reach for the nearest cardboard box with a handle. A paw lashes out at me.

"Be nice! I saved you." I hold the handle with my fingertips, my arm extended.

We line the boxes up at the edge of the tall grass and then Henry opens the cab of the truck, taking out two pair of gloves, handing one to me. "Should've thought of this earlier."

When we've got the gloves on, Henry and I stand at opposite ends of the cat carriers and begin to unfold the lids.

Not a single cat climbs out of their box.

"Cool. Cool, cool," I say.

Henry shakes his head, laughing. "I guess we just let them be and they'll get out when they get out."

"Okay, well I suppose I'll get back to painting," I say. "I'm sure you have better things to do."

He shrugs again. "I meant to ask you yesterday. There's a small biz association meeting tonight. Want to go?"

"Sure, that'd be great. I haven't been to town in a couple days. Shall I drive?"

"Sounds good. Pick me up at 5:30? We can grab a custard beforehand."

Mmm. I've been to Buster's three times now and am working my way through the menu. "It's a date."

Henry winks at me. "If I was taking you

on a date, I'd like to think I could do better than custard and a small biz meeting."

I want to be flirty and inquire more about what a proper date with him would entail, but my mouth momentarily stops performing it's speaking function. My face heating function is in perfect working order, though.

"See ya at 5:30, Let," Henry says, taking the pair of work gloves from my outstretched hand.

"Later, skater."

"À bientôt."

"Aloha."

"Peace."

"Cheerio."

He gets in his stinky truck while I stand there with a goofy smile on my face.

* * *

Henry is waiting for me on his porch, leaning against a post, his legs crossed at the ankles. It's a good look. Let's leave it at that. He stoops to pick something up behind the porch railing and then walks to the car carrying a bag of grocery store brand cat food.

He opens the right side back door and sets

the bag on the seat. "The vet said to put out food and water for the cats three or four times a week in the morning. Just in an aluminum pie pan filled to cover the bottom. Not real near your house." He closes the door and gets in the front seat.

"Got it," I say. "As I was leaving, I checked the boxes, and they were all empty."

"Success!" Henry says, latching his seat belt.

I press play on the CD player before turning the car around.

"Madonna, huh?" Henry asks.

"All right with you?"

He nods. "Your car, your music. Although, I prefer *The Immaculate Collection* over *You Can Dance* as far as compilations go."

* * *

I'm lucky enough to find a parking spot right across from Buster's, which has an epic line as per usual.

Monica and Hunter are waiting off to the side for their order. I give them a wave and Henry nods to them.

"You're here almost as much as we are," Monica says. She leans toward me and lowers her voice. "I'm pregnant again and the baby *needs* custard. I'm fixing to gain sixty pounds this time."

I grin at her. "You gotta do what you gotta do."

"Will we see you all at the meeting this evening?" she asks. "I enjoyed your presentation last time Henry."

He tips his hat.

"Yep. That's our next stop," I say. We move forward in line.

"See you there, then. We're eating and walking." Hunter hands her a cup wrapped in a napkin with a spoon sticking straight out of the top.

"See you."

I get a chocolate cone dipped in cherry, which is my favorite so far – I'll have to let Darcie know – and Henry gets an Oreo concrete. There aren't any free tables at Buster's, so we walk over to the nearby park and sit on a bench underneath a big oak tree people watching, and then drive over to the library.

When we arrive, there's a few people

gathered outside the meeting room door waiting for the librarian to open it.

Henry nudges my arm. "Let me introduce you to Afton Dubois," he nods toward a woman probably in her sixties with a gray bob haircut, wearing a loose navy-blue batik sundress, brown Birkenstock sandals, and green horn-rimmed glasses. "She lives across from you about a quarter mile up the road."

"Oh, nice. She's the photographer I was hoping would take some pictures for my website."

"She actually made the TC Trail Rides site," Henry says.

"Good to know. Your website is great. I'm copying the reservation system."

The door to the room opens and people file in, taking a seat around a long light gray conference table. There's a whiteboard/screen on the wall behind the head of the table, and more stacks of chairs around the room.

Afton sits at the end near the white board. Henry sits next to her, and I snag the seat on the other side of him.

"Afton, this is Lettie. She's the new owner of the Enchanted Cavern Cottages."

The woman smiles at me, and I wait for

the inevitable pity in her eyes, but instead she has a wistful expression. "I'm so happy someone is giving that special place the TLC it deserves. I have fond memories of walking the property and photographing the native plant garden when my friend Miss Lettie was the proprietor."

"That space is a feral cat sanctuary at the moment," I say, testing the idea out.

"I love it!" she exclaims, reaching across Henry and drumming her fingers on my forearm. "I am so sorry I haven't stopped by to welcome you to Tyler Creek, I've been visiting my daughter in Boston. Layla has just had my first grandbaby, Quinn."

"Congratulations," Henry and I say in unison.

"Well, thank you. I'm just thrilled, of course." Her eyebrows raise and she waves to someone. "Buster's here. Have you had a frozen custard from Buster's yet? It's divine."

"We were there right before we came here," Henry says.

"Excellent." Afton puts a hand to her chest. "May I recommend the pistachio concrete with a caramel drizzle? It's to die for."

"I'll add it to my list of locals' favorites," I say, taking out my phone.

"Hey, Afty," says a man who could only be named Buster, as he sits across from Henry. He's got a full head of wavy gray hair and is wearing a hot pink Hawaiian print shirt and khaki shorts.

"How're you, you old coot?" Afton asks, flashing Buster a bright smile.

"Never better, old gal." Buster nods at Henry. "Henry." Then he nods at me. "Lady next to Henry."

"This is Lettie, Buster," Henry says.

Buster slaps his hand on the table. "Yes, it is. You look a lot like another Lettie I used to know."

"My great aunt."

"She's fixin' up the cottages," Afton says.

"Yes, you are. You go girl."

When all the seats around the table are filled, people take chairs from the stacks and plop them down where they stand.

A biracial woman goes to the head of the table, and everyone settles down.

"That's Frankie," Henry whispers to me behind his hand. "She owns the Christmas shop and is the leader of our group."

"Good evening, folks," Frankie says. "It's lovely to see everyone." She looks at me. "New faces, but mostly old."

Everyone laughs.

Buster points to me. "This here's Lettie, everybody. Miss Lettie's great niece."

"She's the new owner of the Enchanted Cavern Cottages," Darcie chimes in from down the table where she sits with Jack, Monica, and Hunter.

Murmurs of 'welcome' and 'Lord have mercy' and 'I'll pray for you' sound around the room.

Henry chuckles and glances at me. "Aren't you glad you came?"

My lips quirk up in one corner. "Thank you for the warm welcome, you all," I say, not quite able to make my mouth say y'all yet.

Frankie picks up a remote control that's Velcroed to the wall next to the white board and powers on the projector hanging from the ceiling. "Tonight's presentation is Curb Appeal for a Steal by Duncan from TC Hardware. After that, Luca and Liv have brought some new items they're thinking about adding to the Fromage brunch menu for a taste test."

Buster claps his hands together. "Yeah, buddy."

Everyone else shares the same sentiment.

* * *

"I actually got a lot out of Duncan's presentation," I say, turning up the AC in the car.

"Who do you think suggested the wine barrel planters in my picnic area?" Henry says. He pats his stomach. "I ate way too many of those mushroom and gruyere crepes."

"I did notice you were gobbling them up," I joke.

He laughs. "Well, I'll work 'em off tomorrow, I suspect. I've got the day off. What's next on your to-do list?"

I pull out of the library parking lot and head towards home. "You don't have things you need to do at your place?"

"I do," he says, smirking, "but I get most of my chores done before you even wake up in the morning."

That earns him some side-eye. "What time do you think I get up?"

"Like seven or so?"

Called out! "Um, yeah. And you're done with your chores before then?"

"I start in on my chores at four a.m. sharp." He turns to look at me. "So, what do you need me to do tomorrow?"

"I've got to pick up an order of laminate flooring at the Home Depot over in Bentonville. You want to come with?"

Henry nods. "Sure. Should we take the truck, though?"

"Yeah, if you don't mind. Otherwise, I'll have to make several trips."

He points ahead of us. "Turn left up here past that collapsed barn." He grins. "Where Afton's going. That's her Prius. Follow her."

"I've never gone this way." I shake my head. "Are you telling me there's yet another way to get to our houses?"

"This is a shortcut. It doesn't make any logical sense and you have cut across Larry Enright's cornfield, but it shaves ten minutes off the drive."

"And Larry Enright doesn't mind?"

Henry snorts a laugh. "Nah. He's the one who told me about it."

Twelve

Henry

"You've got a surprise for me?" Lettie asks, pouring us both an iced tea, the glasses balanced on the freshly painted railing of her front porch.

"I do. It's in the truck," I say, getting up from the porch swing where I'd been breaking in the new blue and yellow striped cushion we'd bought on the second Home Depot run earlier today.

As I stride to my truck, I smile to myself again that Lettie had entertained the idea of hauling eight cottages worth of laminate flooring in her station wagon. It had taken all day to pick up the order in Bentonville, bring it back here, and stack the boxes in cottage four's empty bedrooms so the flooring can acclimate for a few days before she installs it. Either she's horrible at math or she'd never intended to take her car in the first place.

We do this dance often. Lettie needs my help but doesn't want to ask for it but will accept it willingly if I offer. I get it. I'm the same way. Folks like us don't get to be in our forties and still single without a strong independent streak. I have no doubt I will also be learning to install laminate flooring in the near future.

The thing is, I really don't mind. I love spending time with Lettie just doing D.I.Y. or listening to music or shooting the breeze. Nothing fancy, but it suits us both.

Now if I could only get the nerve to kiss her and ask her to be my girlfriend. I'm rusty when it comes to this love stuff, but I seem to recall that after the getting to know you period, the kissing and cuddling portion of the relationship begins. Ideally, that portion never ends.

I slide my black padded guitar case from its hiding place behind the seats underneath a horse blanket.

"Is that what I think it is?" Lettie asks, so close to me I flinch. She laughs. "Sorry."

"You can't wait one minute?" I ask, feigning exasperation. I gesture with the case toward the front porch.

Lettie shrugs. "I can't."

The playful sparkle in her eyes does funny things to my insides. Butterfly things.

We climb the porch stairs and I go back to my seat on the swing while she sits in a well-worn rocking chair she'd dragged up from the basement when she'd finally gathered enough courage to go down there.

No sooner has she sat down than she's up again, grabbing a glass of tea from the railing. "We should've got a little table too."

"I probably have one I can spare," I say, removing my guitar from its case. "My back deck has more outdoor furniture than one person needs."

"Besides," she says, tucking her left foot under her right leg, "I don't imagine you have any time to laze about." She grins.

"What am I doing right now?" I say,

tuning my guitar. "This is textbook lazing about."

"Your textbook must be a second edition because it looks to me like you're about to play the guitar." She says it git-tar in her awful approximation of a southern accent. She's adorable.

"And sing," I say.

Satisfied that the git-tar is tuned, I start playing *Me and Bobby McGee*.

"Busted flat in Baton Rouge..." I sing, my voice a little shaky until Lettie joins in, her confidence bolstering mine.

By the end, Lettie's clapping her hand against her thigh and I'm tapping my foot on the floor.

"Big finish," I say, strumming the final notes.

Lettie places her palm over her heart. "Henry Workman you are the sweetest ma– ...neighbor a girl could ask for." She shakes her head. "I can't believe you play the guitar and sing in addition to all the other things you excel at. Is there anything you can't do?"

I clear my throat. *Hank, it's now or never.* "Find the courage to kiss you? Tell you that since you've been in TC my days are brighter?"

Lettie's mouth drops open. Her gaze locks on mine for a moment, maybe the longest moment of my entire life, then she sets her tea on the floor and, well, Lettie launches herself at me, taking my face in her hands and planting one on me.

All she needed was for me to offer.

When she ends the kiss, Lettie looks down at me while she strokes her thumbs along my jawline. "You make my days brighter too." Tears well in her eyes. "In fact, if it wasn't for you, I wouldn't have survived this long. I would've peaced out to Oregon a month ago."

"So long, sucker?"

She nods and wipes her eyes with the back of her hand. "Arrivederci."

"Hit the road, Jack?" I set my guitar aside, leaning it against the porch railing, and take her hand, pulling her onto my lap.

"Make like a tree and leave." Lettie threads her arms around my neck, resting her head on my shoulder.

"Head on home?" I rub circles on her back.

"I am home," Lettie says.

The sound of tires crunching on gravel and headlights illuminating the tall grass send the cats scattering.

"You expecting someone?" I ask. It's not too late, coming up on eight o'clock, but not exactly regular visiting hours.

Lettie shakes her head and stands up, smoothing her hands down the front of her shirt.

I stand too and move to get in front of her, but she tugs on my shirt sleeve. "I got this. It's okay."

A man dressed in a dark suit exits a white Range Rover and waves to us. "Hello, Ms. Montague? I apologize for the late hour. My GPS was rendered useless, and I got turned around." He chuckles.

Lettie takes a step forward. "The cottages aren't for rent yet. I should have a vacancy at the end of next week, if you're interested in coming back." She walks to the top of the stairs. "That is if you can find the place again."

"May I approach?" he asks, holding up a briefcase. "I have a business proposition."

"Sure. That'd be fine." Lettie slides a glance to me, and I shrug.

"He doesn't look like an axe murderer," I whisper, but not quite low enough the man can't hear me.

"I assure you I'm not," the man says, coming up the steps and extending his free hand toward Lettie. "Giles Pryor, esquire."

She shakes his hand and then looks around the porch. "I'd invite you in, but there's honestly more places to sit out here than in the house."

While she moves to sit on the swing, I step forward holding my hand out. "Henry Workman. I live next door."

Giles gives me a weak handshake and sits down in the rocking chair, setting the briefcase on his knees and opening the lid. He takes out a manila folder and passes it to Lettie. I sit on the swing next to her, crossing an ankle over my knee and stretching my arm along the swing behind her. She rests against me.

"I represent Mr. Chadwick Tate, out of Charleston, South Carolina," Giles says, as if that explains everything.

Lettie opens the folder. I glance over her shoulder at what looks like a contract.

"Am I supposed to know who Chadwick Tate is?" she asks.

"Only if you follow financial news and its key players." Giles closes the briefcase. "I'll not take up more of your time and get right to the point.

Please do. I'm fighting a hard eye roll.

"Mr. Tate would like to purchase your property. He wants to build a residence in the area and your land is an ideal site."

"Oh. No." Lettie closes the folder and makes to pass it back. "Sorry. This place isn't for sale."

"Mr. Tate is prepared to offer two point five million." Giles doesn't take the folder.

"As tempting as the offer is," Lettie begins.

"He'll go as high as three point five, but that is his final offer. Mr. Tate is also looking at another property up the road owned by a Ms. Dubois. Although it's larger, her land is not as favorably situated." Giles stands. "Take a few days to think about it. My contact information is on the first page of the contract."

"Um," Lettie says, and stands, clutching the folder to her chest. "I'll think about it."

My heart races and I want to tell her not to

even think about this. That she said TC is home and we'd just started something good. But I keep my mouth shut. This is not my decision to make.

We watch Giles leave, Lettie waiting until his taillights fade to turn to me.

Her brow furrowed; she sighs. "Three point five million is a lot of money."

I nod. "It is."

"And I wasn't financially prepared to renovate this place to the extent it needs. If I don't start renting cottages three and four in the next three weeks…" Lettie looks away, her shoulders slumping. "I've run through my savings way faster than I anticipated, but I'm staying just one single step ahead."

I stand and take the folder from her, tossing it on the swing. I wrap her in my arms. "You know I'll help you. I'll do whatever it takes to keep you here. You've become someone I can't lose, Lettie."

She tilts her face up to mine. "Can we do the kissing again? Tonight Lettie wants denial and kisses. Tomorrow Lettie can deal with the contents of that wretched folder."

"Tonight Henry concurs," I say, lowering my lips to hers.

Thirteen

Lettie

The next morning, I walk over to Afton's house. The air is heavy with humidity, further weighing down my mood, and the gray skies guarantee rain is coming. Immediately after my visit I'll need to finish patching the hole in cottage three's kitchen roof. I thought I had more time.

The scent of gardenia clings to me as I travel up her gravel driveway. It's much like Henry's – mailbox, little hill, straight drive to the house.

Afton's house is a massive white Greek revival affair, with black shutters and front door, encircled with gardenia. It's not what I was expecting given her appearance the other evening at the small biz meeting.

Four wide concrete steps lead up to the porch which stretches the length of the house. I look around for a doorbell and don't see one, so I take hold of the big, gold lion's head door knocker and give it a thunk thunk.

I hear the flip flip flip of her shoes against her feet coming to the door, so I take a step back off of the mat I've been standing on, that says, 'y'all means y'all.'

Afton flings the door open. Today's outfit is a pink sleeveless drop waist seersucker dress, purple bedazzled flip flops and yellow framed glasses. "Lettie, I thought you might be stopping by today." She waves me into the foyer. The floor is white marble, congruous with the outside of the house, but the walls are painted a kelly green and covered with gold framed color photos of people and flowers and birds. All sorts of interesting subjects.

"How did you know I'd come over? Did Giles give you a visit yesterday too?"

Afton rolls her eyes and hooks her elbow with mine, leading me down a hallway deeper into the house. "Is Giles the new lawyer's name? The last one was Terrence." Afton points to a red banquette by a tall back window in her teal-colored kitchen. "Sit. I'll make some coffee."

I slide into the comfy seat, resting my elbows on the shiny black tabletop, reconsidering my judicious use of bargain off-white paint. Maybe I'll paint my kitchen hot pink. That goes with avocado hued appliances and orange countertops, doesn't it?

Afton fills a reusable coffee pod with grinds and pops it into her Keurig, pressing a button. "To answer your question from earlier," she says. "I was fetching my mail when I saw a white Range Rover driving by real slow, the man at the wheel doing this," she acts like she's gripping a steering wheel at ten and two, her chin jutting over it and her eyes squinting to see, "and I knew the vultures had come circling."

She removes the first bright yellow coffee mug from under the machine, setting it onto the black countertop and repeats the process. "You take anything in your coffee? I've got oat milk, almond milk, milk milk, cream, hazelnut fake creamer stuff, plain white sugar, Splenda, stevia, and Sweet-N-Low."

"I'd love a splash of almond milk and a full packet of Sweet-N-Low." No one ever has Sweet-N-Low. I love my saccharin.

She fixes my coffee and brings it over to the table and then goes back to retrieve hers, which apparently, she takes black.

Afton sits across from me, takes a sip of hot coffee and sighs. "Once a year for the past fifteen, sixteen years, that snake Chadwick Tate sends one of his snively lawyers over here to try to get me to sell my land." She grins. "Henry's dad, Vic, ran the lawyer off on horseback with his shotgun the first year. Of course, Mr. Fancypants Esquire didn't know the shotgun was a replica and couldn't fire, but Vic frightened the man enough that Tate doesn't send anyone over there anymore. Henry was off doing his rodeo thing. He probably doesn't even know about it."

"I don't think so. He seemed as surprised as I was by the visit."

"Henry was there when the lawyer came by?" Afton waggles her eyebrows at me. "Interesting."

I laugh. "I'd say it wasn't like that, but it's totally like that."

She applauds. "Everyone at the meeting the other evening was talking about there being something brewing between you two."

My cheeks heat. "So," I drawl, "why do they keep coming back to your place?" I ask, taking a drink of my coffee.

Afton grins. "I enjoy saying no to men who think they're powerful." She rests back against her seat. "And the lawyers always get lost. It's comical."

"Did Tate ever try to buy my property before? Aunt Lettie had already moved to the nursing home fifteen years ago."

"Oh, he tried. But Miss Lettie's lawyer always kept them at bay."

I scrunch up my nose. "Until I came along."

"Yep. Sorry, honey. Tate is definitely trying to take advantage of you." She drums her fingertips on the side of her mug. "Did this Giles character say that your property was ideal? Offer you three mil?"

"Three point five." I shake my head. "And, yeah, he said that your property is good, but mine is ideal and the one Tate really wants."

"You want a little bourbon for your coffee?" Afton asks. "You look like you might need it."

"No, I'm fine," I say, chuckling.

"Lettie, your property is worth nearly five million dollars, as is mine, as is the Workman's. That fool is lowballing us."

I swallow a mouthful of coffee before I choke. "Okay."

"Not to mention his politics are abhorrent. Pro-gun, anti-LGBTQIA, pays a bunch of lobbyists to keep common sense gun laws from passing." Afton scowls. "There's a picture on the internet of him on a safari with his foot propped up on a dead baby elephant."

My stomach drops. "What! That's got to be illegal."

Afton tilts toward me. "I did some research on Tate's other residences. He's got fourteen all up and down the southeast and every one of them has a huge outdoor gun range. Can you imagine the racket?" She gags. "And the company? No thank you."

"So, Tate's really not the type to let a dozen feral cats stay on his property, then?"

"I'd reckon not."

I look out the window to Afton's back-
yard, the Enchanted Caverns Cottage sign
leaning against the big oak still visible from
here. "Well, that settles it. The money would
come in handy, but the only thing I really
need money for at the moment is fixing up the
cottages." I sigh. "Better to just keep on
keepin' on. A free house to live in is not
nothing."

Afton nods. "Have you thought about
taking a loan out against the property?
Philomena at TC Savings and Loan would
give you a fair shake."

I slump back into the banquette. "Unfortunately, even an unfair loan isn't a possibility. I
co-signed with an ex on an RV a few years
ago and he skipped town to Mexico, leaving
me responsible for payments I couldn't make
on a brand-new Winnebago I'd never even
gotten to take a trip in. I had to declare
bankruptcy."

"Oh, honey. I'm sorry to hear that." She
reaches across and pats my forearm. "Henry
is as solid as they come. He'd never do you
like that."

"No, he won't. Plus, I'm never going to be

that stupid again." I push my coffee away. Thinking about Nick still makes my stomach turn.

Afton looks out the window, her eyebrows drawing together. "What do you think about me taking some photos of your cats? I'd donate the proceeds toward helping you fix up the cottages." She grins. "My work fetches a pretty penny, and I don't even need the money. My late husband left me more than enough to last me and then some."

"You'd do that for me?" I ask.

"Sure, I would," Afton says, waving my question away. "Miss Lettie was a wonderful friend to me after my husband passed. She'd want her gift to you to be a blessing, not a burden."

I let out the breath I'd been holding in. "I don't know what to say, Afton. That's so generous of you."

Afton smiles at me and takes our coffee cups to the sink. "Let me go grab my camera. The light is spectacular right now. All moody and overcast."

I smile back at her, sliding out of the booth. "I hope the cats aren't hunkered down hiding away from the impending rain."

She shrugs. "I'll cut a bunch of catnip from the patch by my studio. That'll flush 'em out."

"Oh, do you have housecats?" I ask, looking around for evidence of kitties.

"Nah," Afton says, looping her elbow around mine. "I just like being prepared. You never know."

I chuckle. "You never do."

Fourteen

Lettie

I awake with a jolt from a dream that I'm on a rowboat sailing across choppy, dark water, wind blowing me to and fro as I paddle furiously. At first, I think I'm still dreaming but then I realize the landline is ringing out in the front room while a raging storm bashes into the roof and sides of the house.

Wrapping a sleeping bag around my shoulders for… protection? I stumble down the hall and rush to answer the phone. The windowpanes in the front room rattle with every strong gust of wind that blasts against the house. Lightning flashes and cracks, illuminating them for a couple seconds before plunging the house back into darkness.

"Hello?" I grip the phone and press it to my ear. The digital clock on the phone charger says 3:14 am.

"Lettie," says Henry, his voice frantic. "Get down to the basement. If you hear a siren, that means there is a tornado coming. Do not got outside. I've got to stay with the horses. I'll come over as soon as I can."

"Uh, okay," I say, pulling the sleeping bag tighter. A zing of terror shoots through me. "Should I... what about the cats?"

The ringing of water spraying into a metallic vessel comes over the line.

"The cats have already found a place to hide, I'm sure," Henry says. "Get to the basement. Please. I can't be worrying about you and do what I need to here."

"Right," I say. "I'm going to the basement right now. Taking the phone with me." I run through the kitchen, drop the sleeping bag to the floor, and yank the basement door open.

"Be safe, Let," Henry says.

"You, too," I say, feeling along the stairwell wall for the light switch.

Henry hangs up and I turn the light on. *Thank God the power's not out.*

I tuck the cordless phone under my arm, grab the sleeping bag, and close the basement door behind me.

There's no furniture to sit on down here as I've taken the only chair up to the porch, and the floor is clammy? Sticky-damp? So, I'm left with the bottom steps or on top of the washer/dryer.

The two windows near the ceiling on the wall behind the washer/dryer shake with the howling wind, giving me my answer.

Just as I'm making a sleeping bag nest on the bottom two wooden steps, the overhead lights flicker and then go out.

Awesome. I know for a fact there isn't a flashlight or any candles down here because when I was doing a load of towels the other day, I'd thought to myself that I needed to get a flashlight and some candles down here in case of an emergency and then promptly forgot about it.

I look up the stairs toward the door to the kitchen. My phone is in my bedroom and it's not that far away, but I'd promised Henry I'd stay in the basement and with my luck, the instant I set foot in the kitchen a tornado would come barreling by.

Through the chaos going on outside, I hear a loud crack and then a boom. I wait to hear the sound again, but don't, and from where I'm sitting, I can't see anything except sideways rain.

Taking a steadying breath, I prop my elbows on my knees and my head in my hands and close my eyes. It's going to be a long night.

* * *

The lights come back on at what I'm guessing is a couple hours later. I have no way of knowing the time, apart from the sky leaking orangish dawn light through the basement windows. The wind has died down and the rain, thunder, and lightning stopped about an hour ago. The tornado siren never did go off.

I call Henry on the cordless phone I've had gripped in my right hand since I came down to the basement, grateful my Millennial brain still has the capacity to memorize phone numbers.

The phone rings and rings, probably eight times, before an answering machine clicks on.

"Thank you for calling Tyler Creek Trail Rides. I'm likely out on the trail or in the stable tending to the horses. Please leave a message and I'll get back to you as quick as I can." And then…beeeeeeeeep!

"Henry? It's Lettie. Call me please. Things have calmed down, so I'm going upstairs. Hope everything is okay with you. Bye."

I climb the stairs, dragging the sleeping bag with me, and emerge into the kitchen. Out the back window I can see the ground is strewn with sticks and larger branches, leaves and the blue and yellow striped cushion that used to be on the porch swing. That sucker had been tied down.

Before I can face what the rest of my property looks like, I go to my bedroom, dump the sleeping bag and phone on the bed, pull on a pair of cutoffs underneath my gray nightshirt, and slip on my red Crocs. Then I use the restroom and brush my teeth, put my hair into a ponytail, wipe my face off with a wet washcloth. Clean my ears. Apply lip balm. Pluck my eyebrows. Switch out the diamond studs in my earlobes for little silver hoops.

"Just get it over with," I say to myself in the mirror, as I'm laying the contents of my shaving kit along the edges of the sink preparing to put on a full face of going out makeup. "It's either a disaster or it's not."

Ever since the loud crack and boom, the idea has been churning in my brain that one of the big trees in the center of the circle drive fell over, either on top of my car or onto the cottages.

Things have been going too well for me. There are the money worries, yes, but what are those compared to Henry and Afton and the beauty of my new home? No way I get out of this storm unscathed.

I keep my eyes down as I walk through the front room and open the front door, then I take a deep breath and lift my head.

A tree has fallen down, a big pine with its roots twisting up into the air, the trunk across the driveway, the top on the ground right between cottages one and two.

My shaky hands fly to my face, covering my gasp.

The tree is a mess, but messes can be cleaned up.

Tires crunch on the gravel as three pickup trucks come down the drive, with Henry in the lead. He parks just before cottage one and the other two park behind him.

Henry smiles and waves and then hops out of his truck. "I drove by earlier and saw the tree. I went to town for reinforcements."

I hurry down the steps, running toward Henry, but stop when I realize there's no easy way to get around or over the tree.

"Give us an hour and we'll get a path cut through. Then I'll kiss your face," Henry says. I can only see him from the shoulders up.

"Who's with you?" I ask, standing on tippy toes to get a look at the 'reinforcements.'

"Darcie's current husband, Jack, and her ex-husband David. They're both contractors. They've got more tools than anyone else I know."

I run back over to the stairs, so I have a better vantage point. Jack and David are hauling chainsaws and tree trimmers out of their trucks.

"You guys like apple pie?" I ask.

Both nod and give me a thumbs up.

"Okay, I'll start baking!"

So, I spend the morning slicing apples and rolling out dough and measuring cups of sweet pickle juice to the sounds of chainsaws and men shouting back and forth at each other, until Henry rushes through the front door, coming straight to me, and kisses my face.

"How's everything at your place?" I ask, when we come up for air.

Henry rests his forehead against mine. "Fine. The horses were a little rattled during the worst of it, but they're good now. There're some branches to clean up in the yard. One of my hanging baskets liberated itself from its hanger and spilled onto the porch. Nothing major." He rubs his callused fingertips up and down my arms. "Nothing like a big ol' pine tree splitting my property in two. I was expecting you to be more shook up."

I shrug. "I've lived through worse. Like the five years before I moved to Tyler Creek."

Henry pulls me into an embrace, and I lay

my cheek against his chest. "Don't get me wrong, I was prepared to throw an epic sobbing hissy fit if that tree had smashed my car or one of the cottages, but as it is, all it destroyed was overgrown landscaping."

"Yoo hoo!" Afton calls from the front door. "Welcome Wagon!" She laughs, joined by two other voices.

"Come on in," I say, disentangling myself from Henry.

He kisses my temple. "I'll leave you ladies to it."

Afton, Darcie, and Monica stroll past Henry on his way out into the kitchen, each carrying a reusable grocery bag that they set on the counter.

"What's all this?" I ask, peering into the bag closest to me, spying pints of Buster's Custard and plastic wrapped wedges of cheese.

The women start unloading the food into my fridge and freezer, passing the items like they're in a water brigade.

"When the power went out," Afton says, stacking the custard three pints high in my freezer, "all this food got the tiniest bit thawed or warmed up." She rolls her eyes.

"It's totally fine, but businesses have to follow regulations and all that, so the girls and I went around and collected stuff in coolers and are divvying it up."

"I hope you're keeping some for yourself," I say, as Monica crams a wheel of cheese into the empty crisper drawer. "It seems like you brought most of it here."

"Well," Darcie says, handing off the last two pints of custard to Afton. "After we collected the food, we got lazy and decided you should have all of it. Besides, Jack said you were baking pie, so we figured pie needs frozen custard to reach its full potential."

"Thirty pints should do it," I say, laughing. I open the cutlery drawer next to the sink and pull out four spoons. "What do you say we bust into four of these while the pies bake, and the men work?"

Monica snatches a spoon from my hand. "The baby thinks that's the best idea you've ever had."

Afton passes out pints while I hand out spoons and paper towels.

"Now do you suppose the boys have removed their shirts?" Afton asks, a twinkle in her eyes. "I do enjoy dinner and a show."

"Afton Dubois!" Darcie says, shaking her head. "I want to be you when I grow up."

We all laugh and make our way out to the front porch. Somewhere along the line Henry has recovered the cushion for the swing. Darcie and Monica double up there, while Afton takes the rocker, and I plop down on the top step.

To Afton's disappointment, the men are all still clothed, but it's still kinda fun to watch them break down such a huge tree.

I'm about halfway through my pint of pistachio praline when I hear more tires on the gravel driveway.

We all turn to look, even the guys, as Giles parks his Range Rover behind the pickups and gingerly makes his way around debris toward the porch.

"Ms. Montague," Giles says, coming to a stop at the bottom of the stairs. "I'm so glad you weathered the storm. They can be quite destructive. Nothing like them out in Oregon, I assume?"

"Oh, we have this whole tree falling over thing," I say, scraping the sides of my pint down. "Only out there, it happens in the wintertime and involves a whole lot of ice." I take an unhurried bite of custard. "Now, in summer, we have wildfires. You all don't have those out here, do you? Or earthquakes? As far as I know, it floods everywhere. Can't escape that."

Giles gives me a limp smile. "Have you given any thoughts to Mr. Tate's generous offer?"

Behind me, Afton snorts. The men have stopped to watch our exchange.

"Yeah, I spent a couple minutes making a mental pros and cons list," I say, setting my pint aside and draping my forearms over my knees. "Unfortunately, it was full of cons much like Mr. Tate's social group. I'm going to pass and ask that you never bother me again."

"Feel free to bother me, though, dear," Afton says giving him a sickly-sweet smile.

Giles sighs and ignores Afton. "Very well, Ms. Montague. I know Mr. Tate will be disappointed, but if you ever change your mind," he pulls a card from the inside pocket of his beige linen blazer and hands it to me, "you know where to contact me."

I take the card and crumple it up. "Will do."

He turns and strides back to his car. As he passes by Henry, my hot cowboy revs his chainsaw and Giles flinches.

"Ooh, that Giles character is not gonna last long," Afton drawls. "Too skittish to work for Tate. I can't wait to see who they send me next year. Lettie, honey, I'll have to sic you on 'em. I could watch you crumple up the fancy embossed cards of ne'er-do-well lawyers all day long."

Fifteen

Henry

Lettie runs the last bead of adhesive along the bathroom wall while I follow behind with the gray rubber wall base, pressing it on a hands-length at a time.

She steps back and caps the tube in the caulking gun. "And with that, cottage eight is done!"

I finish the last press and hold my hand up for a high five. "Go Team YouTube Reno!"

Lettie laughs and slaps her palm against mine.

I stand and crack my back, then take the caulking gun from her and set it on the edge of the newly re-tiled shower stall. We'd gone with a faux river stone look. "Ready?"

"Ready," Lettie says. "Well, I gotta put on socks and longer pants and different shoes and grab a warm jacket and then I'll be ready."

"Why don't I go get the horses and meet you out by the sign in half an hour?"

Lettie grins and nods. "It's a date."

"So it is," I say, giving her a wink.

* * *

Forty-five minutes later, Lettie comes jogging down the driveway, the red cowboy hat I'd given her when the first four cottages were complete listing to the side all cattywhompus.

She rights it, laughing. "Sorry I took so long. Frankie called to chat about the updates to her website and then mentioned Luca and Liv wanted me to revamp Fromage's, so I had to call Liv to set up a time to meet with them and then Chick Reeves had a question about how to use the woodstove in cottage four, and you know how he likes to go on, but thankfully Brenda intercepted and said she'd take him to the wood shed since she was headed there anyhow and show him how to work the stove." Lettie sucks in a deep breath and then gives me a satisfied smile.

"It's all right. The horses and I have been enjoying the fall colors." I dismount Edgar and lace my gloved fingers together to form a step to help Lettie onto Winnie.

"Shoot. I forgot gloves," Lettie says, mounting Winnie in one fluid movement. She probably doesn't need my help anymore, but I like to offer it just the same.

"I've anticipated this and brought a pair for you," I say, grinning up at her.

She pushes down the brim of my hat with a laugh. "You think of everything, my sweet man."

I take the gloves out of Edgar's saddle bags and pass them to Lettie then get on my horse.

We cross the street and follow the Creek Trail. The leaves have changed within the last week, and they really are beautiful. Red, gold, orange, and a burgundy so deep it's almost black. The afternoon sun is bright against the vibrant blue sky stuffed with fat, puffy clouds.

I do the buttons on my flannel-lined denim jacket all the way up and burrow my chin down into the collar. With the clear skies and changing leaves the brisk chill of autumn has arrived as well, the scent of gardenias replaced by the cool, clean aroma of frost on the overturned soil in the hay fields.

We pass by big ol' twisty tree, and alongside the quiet peach orchard. All the farmworkers have gone over to Del's farm to help with the apple harvest.

Lettie hums an ABBA tune, *Fernando* I believe, and I'm happy to let that be our traveling music.

A quarter mile after we enter the woods, Edgar veers to the right and takes us down the Enchanted Cavern Trail. I turn to see Winnie dip her head down to eat a clump of the last of the straggly grass. Lettie gives Winnie a tap with the heels of her Doc Martens. I've yet to get her into cowboy boots but maybe if I get her a nice red pair for Christmas to match her hat, she'll give in. I'd heard Lettie say y'all to Monica the other evening at the small biz meeting, so her Tyler Creek assimilation is almost complete.

When we arrive at the caverns, the picnic

I'd asked Luca to set up for me at a table along the trail is laid out real nice. A red and black checked tablecloth set with black Fiestaware plates and tumblers, shiny silverware, a pair of chunky silver candlesticks, and a large wicker picnic basket off to the side.

"Henry Workman! Sneaky, sneaky." Lettie swings down off of Winnie and loops the horse's reins loosely around a fence post. "I see you've used the plates and cups Maryann brought you." She shakes her head at me. "Get down off that horse so I can kiss your face."

I tip my hat at her. "Happy to oblige."

Once Let's done laying one on me, I get Edgar settled next to Winnie and then join Lettie at the picnic table where she's taking our lunch out of the picnic basket.

"This all looks so good," Lettie says. "Did Luca set this up for you?"

I nod. "Yeah. When he and Frankie were first dating, I'd passed by them having a picnic like this and remembered thinking about the food for the rest of the day."

"And look where they are now. Must have been the picnic." Lettie opens a bottle of sparkling apple cider and pours us each a cup.

We sit down and eat, talking a little in between mouthfuls of delicious food. We don't see another soul the entire time.

"I guess not everyone can have a fancy picnic in the middle of the day on a random Thursday," Lettie says. "We're the lucky ones."

"We sure are." I lift my tumbler in a toast. "To being your own boss."

Lettie raises her glass and clinks it against mine. "To neighbors who save the day so you can be your own boss."

I finish my drink and then take my guitar case out from under the table where Luca had stashed it for me.

"You're just full of surprises today," Lettie says, refilling her cup.

"I may have learned a new song," I say, getting situated on the bench and tuning the guitar.

"In your spare time? Like at three a.m.?" Lettie pulls a plate of cookies out of the basket and takes the plastic wrap off.

"Yep. Pretty much." I start strumming. "Ah, I don't hardly know her," I sing. "But I think I could love her."

Lettie gasps. "Did Maryann tell you I love this song?"

I give her a wink and sing, "Crimson and clover." While I continue playing, I stand and come around the table to sit next to her. "Now you. Next verse."

"Ah, when *he* comes walking over," Lettie sings, leaning her shoulder against mine. "Now, I've been waiting to…" She stands and turns toward me, drumming her fingertips on the sides of her legs. "Henry, you wanna get married?"

I keep playing. "I don't think that's how the song goes, Let."

She scowls down at me. "Yeah, yeah, crimson and clover, over and over."

"Yeah, my, my, such a sweet thing," I sing.

Lettie puts her hands on her hips, her gaze boring into me. "Henry. Workman. Yes or no?"

"I wanna do everything." I stop singing. "Like get married to you, Let."

"Right answer, sweet man," Lettie says, taking my face in her hands and kissing me for a good long time. Eventually, she sits back down. "Now you can finish the song."

"Where was I?" I ask. "I got distracted by my fiancée."

Lettie sings, "What a beautiful feeling."

It sure is. "Crimson and clover."

She smiles at me, her eyes full of love. "Over and over."

Sixteen

Lettie

The newlywed couple can hardly take their eyes off of each other long enough to check-in to cottage six, which Henry suggested we refer to as the honeymoon suite, 'Because who wouldn't want to honeymoon in Tyler Creek?'

He's not wrong. We stayed in town for our honeymoon. Of course, we spent a good part of it watching Jack and David pour the foundation for our new house in the woods between our properties, but it suited us just fine.

I clear my throat, getting the newlyweds' attention. "As I was saying, Tyler Creek has so much to offer." I line up several brochures on the reception desk. "Right next door is Tyler Creek Trail Rides. Down the hill is Enchanted Caverns State Park. You can go tubing on the creek or visit down-town for fantastic shopping and dining. Not to mention the Tyler Creek Community The-atre where you can see a show." I flip the theatre brochure I designed with Afton's photos over and tap my finger on the back. "Oftentimes starring Broadway actor Hunter Lowe!"

The blond woman, Clarissa, raises her eyebrows at her wife, Marta. "Remember when we saw him in the revival of *Chess*?"

"Yeah, but that's more your thing, honey," Marta says with a wink.

I gesture to the photos around the room. "Or you can chill on-site and visit our feral cat sanctuary. We've recently built them an indoor/outdoor shelter. Also, every evening, we have s'mores around the fire pit and on Fridays my husband and I lead a sing-along of hits from the sixties and seventies."

Both women light up.

"Okay, that sounds super fun," Clarissa says.

I scoop the brochures into a neat stack and hand them along with their cottage key to Marta. "Please don't hesitate to ask for anything. Let Enchanted Cavern Cottages be your home away from home."

"Thank you," Marta says. "I can tell we're going to love it here already."

* * *

I hope you enjoyed *Forever My Home*! This is the last book in the Tyler Creek Series, but you can read about Maryann and Luis' love story in *Bright Fire* (Old Town Braverton Book Eight).

Also by Roxie Clarke

Pinwheel Plant Shop

String of Hearts

Calico Hearts

Tangled Hearts

Christmas in Beaverton - Two Holiday Short Stories

Old Town Braverton Trilogy One

Heart of Flame

Bleeding Heart

The Sweetheart Plant

Purple Heart

Old Town Braverton Box Set One

Secondhand Rose Vintage Thrift Shop

Bright Fire

Bright Smile

Bright Day

Shopping for Love in Cataluma

Inking the Deal

<u>Tyler Creek Series</u>

Forever My Favorite

Forever and Always

Forever Merry Christmas

Forever My Home

About the Author

Roxie Clarke writes low-angst sweet and clean small town romance featuring hunky heroes and happily ever afters.

She lives outside Portland, OR with her husband and their five kids. It is loud at her house.

Catch up with Roxie at www.roxieclarke.com

Special thanks to my beta readers J.R. P.N. and S.S.

- facebook.com/authorroxieclarke
- BB bookbub.com/profile/roxie-clarke
- goodreads.com/roxieclarke

Milton Keynes UK
Ingram Content Group UK Ltd.
UKHW020631200524
442968UK00001B/81